Hard Bargain

"Make it easy, Adams," Duffy said. "Give us the thousand."

"Let them have it, Clint!" Loretta said.

"Sorry, I can't do that," Clint said. "They won't be satisfied with it. They think they'll kill me, take the thousand, and then take you back to get them more. Or maybe they'll kill you after they kill me."

"Shut up," Duffy said. He stepped a few feet away from Franks, who stayed where he was. "Give us the money, missy, or we'll kill Adams."

"Just relax, Loretta."

"I'll give you the money!" Loretta shouted.

"I won't," Clint said.

"You're makin' this hard," Duffy said.

"Yeah," Clint said. "On you."

"H-he ain't backin' off, Duffy," Franks said. "We got him two to one and he ain't backin' off."

"Shut up!" Duffy said.

Franks licked his lips and acquired a twitch in his left eye.

"Is a thousand dollars worth dying for?" Clint asked. The question was for either one of them.

"Damn you," Duffy said, and drew.

Clumsily, Franks also went for his gun.

Loretta's sharp intake of breath was audible, followed by two quick shots.

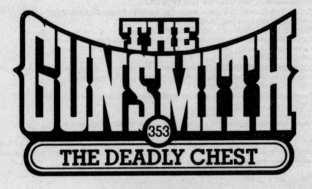

THE GUNSMITH

353

THE DEADLY CHEST

J. R. ROBERTS

J

JOVE BOOKS, NEW YORK

THE BERKLEY PUBLISHING GROUP
Published by the Penguin Group
Penguin Group (USA) Inc.
375 Hudson Street, New York, New York 10014, USA
Penguin Group (Canada), 90 Eglinton Avenue East, Suite 700, Toronto, Ontario M4P 2Y3, Canada
(a division of Pearson Penguin Canada Inc.)
Penguin Books Ltd., 80 Strand, London WC2R 0RL, England
Penguin Group Ireland, 25 St. Stephen's Green, Dublin 2, Ireland (a division of Penguin Books Ltd.)
Penguin Group (Australia), 250 Camberwell Road, Camberwell, Victoria 3124, Australia
(a division of Pearson Australia Group Pty. Ltd.)
Penguin Books India Pvt. Ltd., 11 Community Centre, Panchsheel Park, New Delhi—110 017, India
Penguin Group (NZ), 67 Apollo Drive, Rosedale, North Shore 0632, New Zealand
(a division of Pearson New Zealand Ltd.)
Penguin Books (South Africa) (Pty.) Ltd., 24 Sturdee Avenue, Rosebank, Johannesburg 2196,
South Africa

Penguin Books Ltd., Registered Offices: 80 Strand, London WC2R 0RL, England

This is a work of fiction. Names, characters, places, and incidents either are the product of the author's imagination or are used fictitiously, and any resemblance to actual persons, living or dead, business establishments, events, or locales is entirely coincidental.

THE DEADLY CHEST

A Jove Book / published by arrangement with the author

PRINTING HISTORY
Jove edition / May 2011

Copyright © 2011 by Robert J. Randisi.
Cover illustration by Sergio Giovine.

ISBN: 978-0-515-14938-8

JOVE®
Jove Books are published by The Berkley Publishing Group,
a division of Penguin Group (USA) Inc.,
375 Hudson Street, New York, New York 10014.
JOVE® is a registered trademark of Penguin Group (USA) Inc.
The "J" design is a trademark of Penguin Group (USA) Inc.

PRINTED IN THE UNITED STATES OF AMERICA

10 9 8 7 6 5 4 3 2 1

ONE

When the box fell off the back of the stage, no one noticed.

It was a Concord stage, the type that Mark Twain called "a cradle on wheels." Concords were so well built they never broke down, they just wore out.

But this one was overcrowded. The dedicated luggage rack on top was packed full and strapped down, so some of the luggage had to also be packed on the rear of the wagon.

The Concords rode so well that when they hit the large bump in the road that jolted the black box loose, no one felt it.

The box was solid. When it struck the ground it bounced and rolled, but the lock and the hinges held and when it came to a stop alongside the rode, in a gulley, it was in one piece.

Out in the middle of nowhere . . .

The stage pulled into Westbrook, Arizona, at midday. It stopped in front of the Heritage Hotel, where a worker employed by the California & Arizona Stage Line opened the door. A couple of men piled out, but they went first to make room for the two ladies, who came next. After that, three more men disembarked, and then the worker and the drivers started unloading the luggage. The driver got on top, unstrapped the bags, boxes and trunks and began either handing them or dropping them down.

"Easy with that sample case," the drummer yelled.

He winced as the worker caught the case before it struck the ground, and handed it over.

"Don't drop my jewelry case," one of the women shouted.

The driver handed it down to the other man, who gently turned it over to the woman.

"Thank you," she said, handing him a quarter.

They went to work on the other bags, some of which did slip and strike the ground. Eventually, there was just one woman waiting. She had a bag at her feet, which held her belongings, but she was also waiting for her black chest.

"That's it," the driver shouted.

"Okay," the other man said.

"But . . . wait," the woman called.

Both men froze and looked at her. She was very pretty in her dress, black gloves, and hat. She frowned at both of them.

"Where's my chest?" she asked.

They both looked at her chest, but she didn't notice.

"There was a black box loaded onto the stage in California," she said. "Where is it now?"

"There's no black box up here, ma'am," the driver said. "What did it look like?"

"It was a big, black chest," she said. "I watched you load it on and strap it down on the back."

The driver moved to the back of the stage and peered over.

"What is it, Eddie?" the other man asked.

"I got a broken strap up here, Willie," Eddie Curry said. "I think the box fell off."

"Fell off?" she asked. "But . . . where?"

The driver looked back down at her.

"There's no tellin' where it happened, ma'am."

"Well, we have to go back and look."

"I can't go back, ma'am," he said. "I've got to keep goin'."

"Then how do I find my chest?"

"You'll have to talk to the station manager here in town," Willie said.

"Well . . . can you take me to him?"

"Yes, ma'am," he said, picking up her bag. "Just follow me."

"I'm sorry, Ma'am," Eddie called down. "Go with Willie and I'm sure the manager can help ya."

"I hope so!" she said.

Willie took the woman to the office of the California & Arizona Stage Line office.

"Mr. Blake?"

The man seated at the desk, surrounded by paperwork, looked up at Willie. He was in his fifties, wearing a white shirt with the sleeves rolled up. He had a harried look on his face.

"What is it, Willie?" he asked. "I'm busy."

"I brought a customer in," Willie said, stepping aside so that Andy Blake could see the woman behind him. "She just came in on the stage."

"So?"

"Some of my luggage is missing," she said.

"Damn it!" Blake swore. More paperwork, he thought. "What was it?"

"A trunk," she said. "A large black trunk. Apparently a strap broke and it fell off the back of your stage."

"Well, ma'am—"

"Miss," she said, "Loretta Burns."

"Yeah, well, Miss Burns, have a seat and we'll just fill out a form—"

"A form?" she asked. She approached his desk and slammed her handbag down on it. "Is that all you're going to do? Fill out a form?"

"What else do you want me to do, Ma—Miss Burns?" he asked.

"I want you to send someone out to retrieve my chest," she said.

"And who would you suggest I send out there?" he asked, spreading his arms.

"What about this man?" She pointed at Willie.

"He works here in town," Blake said.

"Then another man."

"I don't have any other men. Besides, where would you suggest they look?"

"Well . . . in the road."

"You mean on the road between here and California? Do you know how long that would take?"

"What about between here and the last rest stop?" she asked.

"Was the chest there at the last rest stop?"

She glared at him. "How am I to know that?" she asked. "Isn't that the responsibility of your men?"

"It's the responsibility of this company to get you where you're goin' safely."

"And not my luggage?"

"Ma'am," Blake said, "we're sorry about your . . . trunk, but there's nothin' we can do but have the next stage be on the lookout for it along the way."

"And will the next stage be along?"

"End of the week."

"I can't wait that long!"

"Well then, I only have two suggestions for you."

"What are they?"

"Get on a horse and go lookin' yerself," Blake said, "or hire somebody to do it for you." He picked up a pencil. "Now, do you want to fill out a form?"

TWO

Clint stared into the mirror while the barber cut his hair. He was covered by a cloth, but underneath he had easy access to his gun. A couple of times, too many young guns had tried to take him while he was in a barber's chair.

"How's it look?" the barber asked nervously.

"Fine," Clint said. "You're doing fine. Just relax."

"Sorry," the barber said. "I ain't never cut a famous man's hair before."

"It's just hair," Clint said.

The barber was thinking, *It's just hair I can sweep up, layer, and sell as the Gunsmith's hair.*

"D-do you want a shave?" the man asked.

"No," Clint said. "I'll take care of that myself."

Clint thought the barber's hand was shaking too much to trust him with a razor.

In a few more minutes, the barber was done. He removed the cloth from Clint and shook it out carefully so that all the hair floated to the floor. He'd sweep it up as soon as Clint left.

Clint stood up, and the barber eagerly used a brush to clean off his shoulders. More hair for the floor.

Clint looked in the mirror nodded, turned and paid the barber, then accepted his hat from the man.

"Thanks," he said.

"Thank you, sir," the barber said. "Bay rum?"

"No, thanks."

"And thanks for comin' into my place."

Clint nodded, headed for the door, then stopped.

"Get a good price," he said to the barber.

"Sir?"

"For my hair," Clint said. "You're going to sweep it up and sell it, right?"

"Uh . . ."

"Just wait until I leave town," Clint said, "and make sure you get a good price."

"Um, yessir."

Clint grinned and left the barber shop.

Outside on the boardwalk he stopped when he saw a crowd gathered in front of his hotel. Seemed to have something to do with the stagecoach that had stopped there.

As he was watching, a man walked up next to him and also stopped to look.

"What's goin' on?" he asked.

Clint looked at him. It was the deputy named Jed Simons. He'd met him several days ago, when he first arrived in town. The sheriff was out of town that day, so Deputy Simons was in charge.

"Damned if I know," Clint said. "Looks like the stage was packed, though."

"Not my worry," the deputy said. "Let Blake worry about it."

"Blake?"

"He manages the stage line here in town," Simons said. "If there's a complaint, he'll have to handle it."

"How about you?" Clint asked. "Handling everything okay?"

Clint looked at the young deputy, who had been left in charge for the first time.

"Everythin's okay, so far, Mr. Adams," Simons said. "And you?"

"Just got a haircut and nobody tried to take a shot at me," Clint said. "That's a good day, so far."

"Yessir. Well, I got to get movin'. See you later."

"In the saloon," Clint said. "I'll buy you a drink when you finish with your rounds."

"Yessir!"

As the deputy walked away, Clint wondered if the young man was even twenty, yet. Sure took a lot of nerve for the sheriff to go off and leave him in charge.

He turned and headed for his hotel.

THREE

By the time Clint got to the hotel, the stage had moved, and so had the crowd. He walked inside and approached the front desk.

"What was all the excitement?" he asked the young clerk.

"One of the passengers arrived without some of her luggage," the man said. "Apparently it fell off the back of the stage."

"Where'd the stage come from?"

"East."

"Will the stage company send someone out to find it?" Clint asked.

"I doubt it," the clerk said. "They don't have anyone to send, and they don't know where it fell off."

"That's too bad. Is she a guest here?"

"Yessir."

"You better make her feel welcome, then," Clint advised.

"That's what my boss told me, sir."

"Then I guess he knows his business," Clint said.

He left the desk and went up to his room. He wanted to change his shirt, because he was itching after his haircut.

Loretta Burns was in her room, pacing back and forth with her arms folded. She needed to freshen up and change her clothes, but all she could think about was the black chest. There had to be some way to find it and get it back.

She needed to hire somebody to do it!

But first she had to have a bath.

She rushed out of the room, almost running into a man in the hallway.

"Oh, I'm sorry," she said, backing up.

"No, no," he said, "my fault."

"Nonsense," she said. "I wasn't looking where I was going. I really don't need your Western good manners at the moment."

"Well," he said, "I'm sorr—"

But she was gone, running down the hall.

Clint watched the pretty woman run off down the hall to the stairway. From her attitude, and the way she was dressed, he assumed this was the woman whose luggage was lost. For that reason alone, he gave her a pass on her bad manners.

"Yes, ma'am," the desk clerk said. "A bath. I can have that drawn for you right away."

"A hot bath?"

"Well . . . yes, ma'am."

"Good," she said. "Send someone to my room when it's ready."

"Yes, ma'am."

"Also, I need to hire a man to do a job."

"What kind of job, ma'am?"

"Would you stop calling me 'ma'am?'" she asked. "It's Miss Burns."

"Yes, ma—Miss Burns. "What kind of job do you need done?"

"I'll discuss that with the man," she said. "Where would I look for someone? In a saloon?"

"Miss Burns, I wouldn't try to go into a saloon alone, if I was you," he said. "You might be taken advantage of."

"Taken advantage of?"

"Someone might take your money and then not do the job."

"Then how do I find someone reliable?"

"Umm, you might try talking to the sheriff?"

"All right," she said, "could you have him come to my room?"

"Um, Ma—Miss Burns, we don't have that kind of control over the sheriff."

"No, of course not," she said. "All right. After my bath I'll go to him. You'll tell me the way, then?"

"Of course, ma'am."

"Thank you."

She turned to run back up the steps and ran into the same man.

"You again?" she demanded.

"Sorry," Clint said. "I didn't expect you—"

"You should just look where you're going!" she said, and ran past him.

Clint walked to the front desk.

"That her?" he asked.

"What? Oh, yes, Miss Burns. She's quite upset."

"I can see that," Clint said. "Must have been something important to her in her luggage."

Clint left the lobby before the clerk could decide to tell him Miss Burns was looking to hire somebody.

FOUR

Sheriff Tom Lane looked up when his office door opened, then jumped to his feet when he saw the woman enter.

"Are you the sheriff?" she asked.

She was so pretty that at first he couldn't find his voice.

"Y-yes, I'm, Sheriff Lane. W-what can I do for you, ma'am?"

"My name is Loretta Burns," she said. "I prefer 'Miss Burns' to 'Ma'am.'"

"Yes, Ma—yes, Miss Burns."

"May I sit?"

"Please do."

Loretta Burns looked and smelled like she was fresh from a bath. At fifty, Tom Lane was still hopelessly tongue-tied around women—especially pretty ones.

"Sheriff, I came in on the stage this morning; when we arrived, one of my pieces of luggage was missing. It was a large, black chest and it had apparently fallen off in transit."

"That's too bad."

"Yes, it is," she said. "That chest is very important to me."

"Well, what is the stage line gonna do about it?" he asked.

"Nothing!" she said. "Absolutely nothing! It's terrible. They refuse to even send a man out to look for it."

"Well, I—I guess they figure, where would they look?" he said.

"Now you sound like that little man who runs the stage line, what's his name? Blake?"

"Yeah, that's his name, Blake."

"Well," she said, "I just cannot accept that there's nothing I can do."

"Well, ma'—um, Miss Burns, I don't see how I can help ya. I can't leave town to go out lookin' for it, and I can't send one of my deputies—"

"I don't expect you to do anything," she said. "I would like to hire someone to go out and look for it."

"Well, you can do that," he said.

"I don't know who to hire," she said. "I was hoping you could steer me toward someone reliable."

"Well," he said, scratching his bald head, "I guess you could go over to one of the saloons—"

"I thought of that," she said. "The desk clerk at the hotel recommended against my going into a saloon alone. He seemed to think I might be taken advantage of by someone . . . disreputable."

"Well, sure," the sheriff said, "There's any number of men who would take your money, go out and have a nap somewhere, and then come back and tell you they couldn't find it."

"What kind of a man would do that?" she demanded.

"A lowlife, miss," he said, "and there's plenty of them around."

"Then what do you suggest I do?" she asked. "Surely you must know someone you can recommend?"

"Well, I can give it some thought," he said. "Where are ya stayin'?"

"The Heritage Hotel," she said.

"Well, lemme think about it and get back to ya," he said.

"I'd like to get someone to go out tomorrow and start looking," she said.

"Well . . . how much would you be willing to pay?"

"One hundred dollars."

He swallowed hard. That was just over two months' salary.

"Ma'am," he said, "don't go sayin' that out loud around town. Just wait 'til you hear from me."

"Very well," she said, standing up. "If I can't trust the local law, who can I trust?"

FIVE

"If she's got a hundred dollars to spend, then she'd got more than that."

Sheriff Tom Lane was sitting in a small stable on the southern edge of town, talking to two other men named Joey Votto and Angel Pagan.

"So?" Angel asked. "How do we get it from her?"

"I'll recommend you to do the job she needs done," Lane said. "You and Joey just wait for her to take her money out to pay."

"And then we take it?" Joey asked.

"Or find out if she's got even more," the sheriff said.

"And she's gonna trust us because you say so?" Angel asked.

"She even said when she was in the office: 'If you can't trust the law who can you trust?'"

All three men laughed.

"Is she good-lookin'?" Angel asked.

"Oh, yeah," Lane said. "She's very pretty."

"So, once we get the money . . ."

"As long as I get my cut," Lane said, "I don't care what you do."

Angel and Joey exchanged a satisfied glance.

Early on in his stay, Clint had chosen the Golden Palace as his saloon of choice. After two beers, he came out of the saloon and took a deep breath. Across the street he saw Sheriff Lane come out of a stable, followed by two other men who looked suspicious. The two of them had worn trail clothes on, and guns worn low on their hips in a fashion they mistakenly thought would allow them to draw their weapons faster.

It looked to Clint like a meeting nobody was supposed to know about.

He stepped back into the saloon and watched through the window as the two men crossed toward him. Obviously they were going to follow up their meeting with a drink.

Clint moved to the end of the bar farthest from the window.

"'nother one?" the bartender asked.

"Why not?"

"Thought you were leavin'."

"Got thirsty on my way to the door."

The bartender laughed and set another beer down in front of him. "It's slow, so I can always use the business," the man said.

The two men entered and immediately walked to the bar. They positioned themselves near the center, so Clint was able to hear their conversation. One of them looked Mexican, the other one white. In his mind, he dubbed them "Mex" and "Gringo."

"Whaddaya think?" Mex asked.

"Lane hasn't steered us wrong yet," Gringo replied. "If he says the woman has money, she has it."

"Which means," Mex said, "that we will soon have it."

"All we gotta do is get her to hire us," Gringo said.

"And if she's as good-lookin' as the sheriff says she is, we can have some enjoyment later," Mex said.

The two men laughed, then quieted down when the bartender came over with two beers.

Clint nursed his beer as the two men continued to talk, but they had lowered their voices, probably to keep the bartender from overhearing.

The two men finished their beers, then slapped each other on the back and left. Clint waved the bartender over.

"Who were those two?"

"Them?" the bartender asked, jerking his thumb toward the spot where the two men had been standing. "That's Angel Pagan and Joey Votto."

"And who are they?"

"Just two troublemakers who hang around town."

"What do they do?"

"Hire out."

"For what?"

"Anythin', as long as it's not honest work," the bartender said.

"And what's their relationship to the sheriff?" Clint asked.

"Um, he's thrown them in jail once or twice for drunkenness."

"That's it?"

"As far as I know."

"So they'd never do an honest day's work for an honest day's pay?"

"Hell, no!"

"Okay, thanks." Clint finished his third beer and pushed the empty mug away.

"Another?" the barman asked.

"No. This time I'm done. See you later tonight, though."

Clint left the saloon, looked both ways for the two men, but they were gone.

Looking for trouble, he was certain.

SIX

When the knock came at her door, Loretta Burns hurriedly opened it.

"What?" she asked the desk clerk.

"Ma'am—I mean, miss, uh, there are two men down in the lobby who want to talk to you."

"What do they want?"

"They say they heard you were hiring."

"Tell them I'll be right down."

"Yes, miss."

She closed the door in the clerk's face. She had to change her clothes for a meeting with potential employees.

"What'd she say?" Angel asked the clerk.

"She'll be right down."

"Good," Joey said.

The clerk stared at the two men.

"What, Dwight?" Angel asked.

"You ain't gonna do nothin', are ya?" Dwight the clerk asked.

"Whadda you care, Dwight?" Angel asked. "You just keep yer mouth shut, ya hear?"

"Uh, yeah," Dwight said, "yeah, I hear."

"Go on back to yer desk," Joey said.

Dwight went.

When Loretta came down, she found two unkempt men waiting for her in the lobby. She had hoped to do better, but in looking around town she found that these two were pretty much representative of the men around there.

"Are you the men looking for work?" she asked.

The two men looked her up and down and made her feel like a piece of meat.

"We heard you was lookin' for some good men," one of them said. He was tall, dirty, and looked Mexican.

"I was looking for one man," she said, "but I could use two."

"You payin' a hundred dollars each?" the other man asked. He was shorter, and white, but as dirty.

"I will pay you one hundred and fifty dollars for both of you," she said. She waited, then added, "That's seventy-five dollars each."

The men exchanged a glance.

Clint was about to enter the hotel when he saw Loretta Burns in the lobby talking with two men—the same two he'd seen in the saloon.

He paused, took a step back, but was still able to watch and listen . . .

"I need you to find something for me," she told the two men.

"What?" Angel asked.

"A trunk, a black trunk."

"How big?" Angel asked.

"Big enough for you to fit in, if you could pull your knees up to your chest."

"Where is it?" Joey asked.

"If I knew that, I wouldn't need you," she told him. Her tone said he was an idiot.

"I think what my partner means is, where did it get lost?"

"It fell off the back of the stage I came in on," she said. "And before you ask, I don't know when it fell off."

"Then how do we find it?" Joey asked.

"I suggest you ride back over the stage route," she said, "and look."

"That could take a long time," Angel said.

"I'll make you a deal," she said. "If you don't find it by the time you get to the first station, I'll double the money."

"This trunk," Angel said, "it must be pretty important to you."

"Sentimental value," she said.

"We will need some money," he said. "We'll need to get outfitted."

"Outfitted?"

"We'll need supplies, since we'll be on the trail for a while."

"Oh, yes." She reached into her purse, "Will fifty dollars be enough?"

"Fifty'll do . . . for now," Angel said.

Clint watched as the woman went back upstairs, and the two men headed for the door. Clint backed up, sat down in a chair he bumped into, and pulled his hat down over his face.

The two men came out, stopped on the boardwalk.

"We got fifty dollars," Joey said.

"So?" Angel asked.

"What do we do?"

"What we said we were gonna do," Angel said. "Get outfitted."

"But the sheriff—"

"The sheriff thinks small, Joey."

"And we don't?"

"I don't," Angel said.

"What are we gonna do?"

"We're gonna find that chest," Angel said.

"What for?" Joey asked. "I thought we was just gonna take her money? And have some fun. She looks pretty tasty, don't she?"

"Yeah, she does," Angel said, "but she sure is anxious to get that chest back."

"Yeah, so? What do you think is in that trunk, Angel?" Joey asked.

"That's what I wanna find out, Joey," Angel said. "That's what we both gotta find out."

SEVEN

Clint watched the two men walk away, remained seated on his chair. This wasn't any of his business. The rude woman had hired two untrustworthy men to find her lost chest. So what if they took her money under false pretenses. What did that matter to him?

For one thing, the sheriff had tipped them off. That made the sheriff crooked, and he didn't like crooked lawmen.

Second, from what the two men had said in the saloon, they were going to do more than just take her money. It sounded like they wanted to rape her. And he hated rapists, more than crooked lawmen. Even if the woman was rude.

And third . . . well, there wasn't a third. Those two things were enough for him to butt in.

He got out of the chair and entered the lobby. Before going up the stairs, he stopped at the front desk.

"You know those two?" he asked.

"Um, what two?"

"The two men who just left."

The clerk looked frightened.

"What's your name?" Clint asked.

"Dwight."

"Well, Dwight, I just need some simple answers. Why would you be too afraid to give them to me?"

"Um, those two, they're—well . . . bad."

"What are their names?" Clint asked, double-checking the information he'd gotten from the bartender.

"Angel and Joey," Dwight said. "I-I don't know their last names."

That was good enough.

Clint went up to the second floor and knocked on the door to Loretta Burns's room. When she opened the door she glared at him. He was amazed a woman could still be so beautiful with such an angry look on her face.

"You!" she said. "Have you come to my own room to knock me over?"

"No, ma'am, I came here to help you."

"With what?" she asked. "I don't need any help."

"If you'd let me come in—"

"You cannot enter my room, sir," she said. "I don't even know who you are."

"My name is Clint Adams."

"That means nothing to me."

He studied her face and knew she was telling the truth.

"Ma'am, I've been hearing around town that you need to hire somebody to find something for you."

"So that's it," she said, folding her arms. "You heard I was offering one hundred dollars for a job and you're here to try and get it. Well, you're too late. I've already hired two men for the job."

"Yes, I know," I said. "I know who they are. Angel and Joey . . . something."

"You don't know their last names?"

"Do you?"

They stared at each other.

"I'm sorry, Mr. Adams," she said. "I've already hired my men. I can't use you."

"The men you hired are, for want of a better word, crooked."

"And you're not?"

"I'm as honest as the day is long, Miss Burns," Clint said.

"I'm sure. I think I'll stick with the men I already have."

"If you do, you'll end up penniless, and raped."

"You're trying to frighten me, Mr. Adams."

"You should be frightened, Miss Burns."

"I can take care of myself."

"Angel and Joey are bad men, Miss Burns, pure and simple," he said. "There's no other way to put it."

"I see. And you want to save me from them?"

"No."

"No? Then why are you here?"

"Just to warn you," he said.

"Well, do you have any other warnings for me?" she asked.

"As a matter of fact, I do," he said. "Don't trust the sheriff."

"What? Why not?"

"Because he sent you those two men," he answered. "Whatever money they get off of you, they have to split with him."

"With the sheriff," she said.

"Yes."

"The law."

"That's right."

"Then how can he keep his job?"

Clint shrugged. "He must have connections in town."

"So you're telling me the town lawman is crooked, the men I hired are crooked, and you're not."

"Now you've got it," Clint said. "I'll say good-bye, now."

"B-but—"

He turned and walked down the hall, quickly down the stairs, and out of the hotel.

EIGHT

If she didn't want his help, there was no point in trying to force it onto her.

This was supposed to be his last full day in town. He intended to ride out in the morning. He had to outfit himself for a couple of days on the trail, and check to make sure his Darley Arabian was in shape to travel. Eclipse had been a little sluggish and feeling under the weather when they arrived.

He walked to the livery stable and found Harley, the attendant, working on a horse's shoes.

"How's he doing?" he asked.

"Your big stallion? He's fine. In the pink, in fact," Harley said. "You ready to go already?"

"Time to move on," Clint said. "I'll just take a quick look at him."

"Go ahead. I've got to get this old boy shoed."

"What is somebody as educated as you doing working in a livery stable?"

"I beg your pardon," Harley said. "I own the livery stable."

"And what did you do before this?"

"I was a schoolteacher."

"Really? Where?"

"Back east. I'm also fifty years old, and very happy with what I'm doing with my life, at the moment. Any other questions?"

"Just one," Clint said. "How about letting me buy you a beer before I leave town?"

"When?"

"Four o'clock? The Golden Palace?"

"I'll be there."

"Good."

He walked into the livery, in the back, where Eclipse stood still in a stall.

"How you doing, big boy?" he said, slapping the horse's muscular rump. "You feeling okay?"

Eclipse shifted about a bit and his big head went up and down, as if he was nodding.

"You're not really nodding, right?" Clint asked.

The horse stood still.

"Right."

Then Eclipse shook his head.

"Okay," Clint said. "You're fine. I'll see you in the morning."

He patted the horse's neck and backed out of the stall.

"Whatever you did to him, Harley, he looks very refreshed."

"He just needed some rest. My guess is you push him pretty hard."

"Yeah. Hey, I got a question."

"What?"

"You know two guys named Angel and Joey?"

"I know Angel Pagan and Joey Votto. Those the two?"

"They together all the time?"

"They are. They're bad men."

"I just told somebody that," Clint said. "Glad to hear I was right."

"You going to get involved with those two?"

"I don't think so. Why?"

"They'd just as soon kill you as look at you," Harley said. "And if they find out who you are, they definitely will try to kill you."

"I'll keep that in mind," Clint said. "Thanks for the advice, Harley."

"Sure," the liveryman said. "See you at four?"

"See you."

Clint started to walk away, then stopped and turned.

"You think they'd kill a woman?" he asked.

Harley looked at him.

"Good-looking?"

"Yes."

"She got money?"

"Yes."

"In a minute," Harley said, "but they'll rape her, first."

NINE

"Are we really gonna go out lookin' for that box?" Joey asked Angel.

"Yes, we are. I tol' you," Angel said, "I want to see what's in it."

"We gonna tell the sheriff?"

"No."

"He ain't gonna like it."

"Then maybe we kill him."

"Kill a lawman?"

"Not the first time," Angel reminded his partner.

"First time in a while, though," Joey said.

They had outfitted themselves with just enough supplies to carry between them. They'd be riding out in the morning. At the moment they were sitting at a table in the Golden Palace, sharing a bottle.

"What the—" Joey said. "Look at that."

Angel turned and saw the woman, Loretta Burns, coming through the batwing doors.

"What is she doin' here?" Angel said.

She spotted them and started over.

"Lookin' for us, I guess."

"You two," she said, stopping at their table.

"Miss Burns," Angel said. "Do you want a drink?"

"No, I don't want a drink. I want my money back."

"But . . . why?"

"You didn't tell me that the two of you were crooks," she said.

"Crooks?" Angel looked at Joey, who shrugged.

"Crooks," she said. "Thieves . . . outlaws, I believe they call you."

"Who told you that?"

"A man named Clint Adams."

Now when Angel looked at Joey, Joey looked worried.

"I know who Clint Adams is," Angel said. "What I don't know is why he would tell you such a thing. He does not know me, or my partner."

"Well, I guess he heard it around town," she said. "And I suppose I should have asked more questions before I hired you. I want my money back."

"Fifty dollars?" Angel asked. "We do not have fifty dollars."

"Where is it?"

"We spent it, on supplies," Angel said.

"Okay," she said, "so we'll go back to the store, give back the supplies, and get me my money back."

Angel thought that over, then said, "No."

"No?"

He stood up, grabbed Loretta Burns by the throat, and said, "No."

"She went where?" Clint asked the clerk.

"To the saloon."

"Which saloon?"

"The Golden Palace?"

"She went to the Golden Palace, or she didn't?" Clint asked.

"She did," Dwight said. "She went to the Golden Palace."

"Why?"

Dwight shrugged.

"Dwight."

"She asked me where I thought she could find Angel and Joey."

"Great," Clint said, running out of the hotel, "just great."

"Hey!" the bartender called.

"Shut up!" Angel said.

"Take it outside," the barman said.

None of the other patrons were paying much attention. Loretta couldn't breathe. She thought this man was going to strangle her to death, and no one was going to do anything about it.

"Okay," Angel said to Joey, "let us take it outside."

"Out front?" Joey asked.

Angel shook his head. "Out back."

They dragged her through the saloon and out the back door. There, Angel released her and pushed her down to the ground.

"How dare you—"

"If you say another word," Angel said, "I will kill you."

She clamped her mouth shut.

"Get her bag," Angel said to Joey.

Joey grabbed her purse, pulled it away from her, and gave it to Angel. It had a drawstring. He opened it, reached in, and came out with a roll of bills.

"Oh, man!" Joey said. "How much is there?"

"I don't know," Angel said. "We'll count it later."

"Later?"

"After."

"After what?" Loretta asked, in spite of herself.

Both men looked down at her and grinned. Then Angel reached down and grabbed her right breast.

Clint ran into the saloon, looked around, then went to the bar.

"Where are they?" he asked the bartender.

"Where's who—"

Clint grabbed the front of the man's shirt. "Don't play games with me! I'm not in the mood."

"They took her out back."

"And you didn't stop them?" Clint turned and looked at the half-full room. "None of you tried to stop them?"

Most of the men looked away. Some of them never looked at him, at all.

He released his hold on the bartender's shirt and headed for the back.

TEN

They had Loretta's shirt open and were pawing her naked breasts when he came out the door.

"Hold it, boys," he said. "Fun's over."

Angel stood up and turned to face Clint. Joey kept trying to grab Loretta's chest.

"Call him off, Angel," Clint said, "or I'll kill him."

"Kill him," Angel said, "and I will kill you. Then I'll have the woman, and the money, to myself."

"Hey!" Joey said.

"Well then, stand up and face him!" Angel said. "Leave the woman for later."

Joey stood up. Loretta pulled her shirt closed and crawled a few feet away, until her back was against a wooden fence.

"T-they were going to rape me," she said. "They dragged me out of the saloon and nobody stopped them."

"Welcome to the West, Miss Burns," Clint said, "where people mind their own business. Now keep quiet."

"Why don't you try mindin' your own business, Adams?"

"Why don't you and your friend walk away, Angel?"

"We work for the lady," Angel said. "She came back here with us willingly."

"Is that true, Loretta?" Clint asked.

"No!" she said, her eyes wide.

"Then why don't you get up and come over here with me," he said.

She quickly got to her feet and ran over to stand behind Clint.

"You boys object?"

"I on—" Joey started, but Angel stopped him.

"Go ahead, take 'er," he said. "There ain't enough meat on her bones, anyway."

"W-what about my money?" Loretta asked.

"How much?" Clint asked.

"Fifty dollars," Angel said. "She paid us fifty dollars."

Jesus, he thought.

"Let it go, Loretta," he said. "Fifty dollars isn't enough to—"

"They took a thousand dollars from me." She clutched her bag. "They took it from my bag. He has it." She pointed at Angel.

"Give it up, Angel."

"We ain't got—" Joey started.

"Just toss it over, Angel," Clint said. "Let's have everybody walk away from this."

Angel hesitated, then took out the roll of cash and tossed it to Clint, who caught it left-handed. He handed it back to Loretta, who clutched it.

"Just back away, into the building."

"O-okay."

"I'll kill the first man who touches his gun," Clint said.

Angel watched Clint, and Joey watched Angel. Clint knew if Angel went for his gun, Joey would follow. He'd have to take Angel first.

But the Mexican never moved, and eventually Clint was inside. He slammed the door, then turned and almost slammed into Loretta.

"Let's go," he said, turning her around. "Through the saloon."

"Through there?" she asked. "But those people—"

"—will mind their own business," Clint assured her. "Go!"

She moved and he followed. They walked through the saloon and out the front doors. Clint was ready in case Angel and Joey had run around front to catch them, but the pair was nowhere in sight.

"Are you all right?" he asked.

"Yes," she said, "just slightly humiliated. Thank you for saving me."

"We better get you back to the hotel so you can change your clothes."

"Then I want to report those men to the sheriff."

"Are you sure?"

"Yes. Will you take me there?"

"Well," he said, "this should be interesting."

ELEVEN

Clint took her back to the hotel and waited while she changed her shirt.

When she came out he asked, "Do you still want to see the sheriff?"

"Definitely. I want those two arrested."

"Just remember what I told you about the sheriff," he told her.

"I can't believe that," she said. "He's the law."

After what had just happened, he couldn't believe her attitude hadn't changed.

"Would you please take me to the sheriff's office?"

Well, maybe it had changed a little.

"Okay," he said. "Come on."

When they entered the sheriff's office Clint was happy to see that Sheriff Lane was around, but Deputy Jed Simons was there.

"Hey, Mr. Adams," Jed said. "Time for that drink?"

"Is the sheriff here, please?" Loretta asked the young deputy.

"Uh, no, ma'am," Simons said. "But I'm the deputy. Can I help you?"

"Deputy, this is Miss Loretta Burns. Just arrived in town this morning on the stage."

"Welcome to town, Ma—"

"I want two men arrested," she said. "They tried to rape me."

"What? Who?"

"Their names are . . . Joey and . . . and . . ."

"Angel," Clint prompted her.

"Right," she said. "Joey and Angel. I don't know their last names."

"Joey Votto and Angel Pagan?" Simons asked.

"Yes," she said. "Arrest them! They dragged me behind the saloon and pulled my clothes off—and no one in the saloon would help me."

"You went into the saloon? Alone?"

"Yes," she said. "I had to get my money back."

"Your money?"

"I paid them for a job, but then I decided I wanted my money back."

"How much?" Simons asked.

"Fifty dollars."

"For what?"

"Why is that important?" she asked. "Do you allow men to rape women at will in the West?"

"At . . . what?"

"Rape is not allowed in the West, Miss Burns," Clint assured her.

"Well then, make this young man arrest those two men," she demanded.

"I can't make him do anything," Clint said. "He works for the town."

She turned to face Clint. "Those two men seemed frightened of you," she said.

"They weren't frightened," he said. "They were careful."

"Why didn't they just produce their guns?" she asked. "I don't understand."

"They wouldn't be crazy enough to throw down with Clint Adams," the deputy said.

Now she looked at him.

"Why? Who is he?" she asked, pointing at Clint.

"Ma'am?" the Deputy said. "Everybody knows who he is. He's the Gunsmith."

"The . . . Gunsmith? What is that, his job?"

"Ma'am, he's a legend," Simons said. "With a gun. Nobody's ever beaten him. He's killed—"

"Okay, that's enough," Clint said.

"A famous gunman?" she said, looking at him. "Then why didn't you kill them?"

"I didn't have to kill them."

"But they were raping me!"

"Well," he said, "actually, they were robbing you, and pawing you, but they hadn't gotten to rape."

"Yet!" she said. "They pulled my shirt open! And you're right, they did rob me. They took a thousand dollars."

"A thousand?" the deputy said. He'd never seen that much money. "Did you get it back?"

"Yes, Mr. Adams got the money back for me. But that's beside the point. If you can't go and arrest them, I want to talk to the sheriff."

Clint watched Jed Simons's face, and was convinced that the young man knew that Sheriff Lane was connected to Angel and Joey. He was stuck in the middle.

"Deputy, why don't you tell the sheriff we were here, and tell him he can find Miss Burns at the Heritage Hotel. She wants something done, officially."

"Uh, okay, Mr. Adams," he said. "I'll do that."

"Thank you."

"But—"

"Let's go," Clint said to Loretta. "You can talk to the sheriff about it later."

"B-but he's a deputy," she protested. "He should be able to do something!"

"Come on, Miss Burns," Clint said, steering her to the door.

Outside, she dug her heels in.

"Why did you do that?" she demanded. "He has to arrest them before they get away."

"He's stuck in the middle, Miss Burns," Clint replied. "He's young, and he knows his boss is connected to those two."

"I can't believe this!" she said. "Nothing will be done?"

"The sheriff will come over and talk to you," he said. "You'll find out then."

"And what about you?"

"What about me?"

"I'll give you this thousand dollars to kill them," she said.

"What?"

"Today," she said. "Right now. Go over and . . . gun them down."

"You're crazy, lady."

"Isn't this the Wild West?" she asked. "Where a woman can't walk into a saloon without being raped?"

"You didn't belong in that saloon," he told her. "Certainly not alone."

"This is the famous Gunsmith?" she asked. "Won't take a thousand dollars?"

"Not to kill someone."

"Isn't that what you do?"

"You don't know anything about me," he said. "You better get over to your hotel and wait for the sheriff."

"Bu—"

He turned and walked away.

"Where are you going?"

He ignored her.

"You can't just leave me here alone."

He kept walking.

"Damn you!"

She looked around, suddenly very frightened to be on the street alone. Two men passed and stared at her, and she immediately panicked and started running back to the hotel.

TWELVE

"Sheriff Lane ain't gonna like this," Joey said to Angel. "We should go after them."

"You wanna face Clint Adams in the street, my friend?" Angel asked.

"Well, no . . ."

"Then keep quiet," Angel said. "Let me do the thinkin', huh?"

"Okay, so then what do we do?"

"Nothing," Angel said.

"What about the woman?"

"We will get her."

"She sure had some nice tits," Joey said. "And her skin was real smooth."

"I know," Angel said. "I think I will go over to Maisie's."

"Now that sounds like a good idea," Angel said. "That woman sure got me worked up."

A whore sounded like a good idea to both of them. Clint Adams had interrupted them before they could get any satisfaction, and Joey was right, Angel thought. The woman had a nice body.

They would see the rest of it another time.

And take care of Clint Adams.

Clint knew he couldn't leave the woman to her own devices, especially not now. Angel and Joey would come looking for her again, and it was possible that Sheriff Lane might take part in killing her, to ensure her silence about his involvement.

And then there was her black box. Whatever was in it might turn out to be valuable. With her dead, the three men could go out and look for it at their leisure.

Damn it.

He stopped walking, trying to decide whether he should go have a beer or return to the hotel. Getting involved in her trouble was going to keep him from leaving town in the morning.

Maybe, he thought, he should just leave town right now.

He decided to go and have a beer and think it over. No point in making any spur-of-the-moment decisions.

Sheriff Lane returned to his office, found young Jed Simons sitting behind his desk.

"Move your ass!" he ordered.

"Yessir."

"Anything happen while I was out?"

"Uh, yessir. Clint Adams came in with a woman who claimed Angel Pagan and Joey Votto tried to rob and rape her."

"What?"

"She wants them arrested."

"Jesus Christ!" Lane said.

"I didn't know what to do," the deputy said. "I know that you and them are . . ."

"Are what?"

"Well . . . friends."

"What the hell, Jed," Lane said. "If they tried to rape somebody, you should have gone out and arrested their asses right away."

"Yessir. I can go out and do that now—"

"Never mind," Lane said. "You had your chance. Where are they now?"

"Adams said the woman would be at her hotel, if you wanted to talk to her."

"Hell, yeah, I wanna talk to her."

He got up from his desk and headed for the door. "I'll be back later," he said. "Stay the hell away from my desk!"

THIRTEEN

At the whorehouse, Angel picked a tall, lean blonde girl, while Joey picked a buxom Mexican woman.

"You don't like Mexican women?" Maisie asked Angel.

"I have had many Mexican women," he told her. "Now my taste is blonde *gringas*."

They both followed the women up the stairs to the second floor. Joey couldn't keep his eyes off his whore's big ass as it swayed back and forth in front of him.

Angel, already excited by Loretta Burns's pale skin, had chosen the palest woman he could find.

They walked down the hall and followed their whores into their respective rooms, which were across the hall from each other.

Both doors slammed.

Joey was anxious, and practically tore his whore's clothes off.

"You are in such a hurry, hombre."

"I wanna see those big tits," he said. "Show me those big tits."

She let him peel off her peasant blouse so that her breasts came tumbling out. They were round, solid, and tipped with dark brown nipples, which she squeezed for him.

He took his own clothes off then, and his rigid cock came swaying into view.

"El hombre *grande*," she said. "*Bueno*, bring it to me, hombre. Bring it here."

She sat on the bed and slipped off her skirt. This was something Joey liked about Mex women, that big, black bush between their chunky legs.

"Oh," he said, "I'll bring it to you, all right . . ."

In the other room, Angel peeled his whore's clothes off more slowly. He wanted her pale skin to come into view little by little.

"Are you always this gentle?" she asked him.

"No," he said. Her breasts were small, with pink nipples. He'd seen Loretta Burns's nipples briefly. They were darker, and her breasts were bigger. But her skin, it was this pale.

The whore's name was Debbie. She put her hands on his belt, but he brushed her hands away.

"Slow," he said. "I wanna go slow."

"We can go slow, mister," she promised him. "We can take all day."

He took one of her breasts in his big hand, squeezed it, and bent to run his tongue around her nipple.

"Ooh," she said, "that's nice. That's so nice."

Most men just wanted to get her clothes off and fuck her, then roll off and go to sleep. This was going to be nicer, much nicer . . .

FOURTEEN

Sheriff Lane entered Maisie's; immediately, all the girls turned their eyes away.

"Sheriff, how nice," Maisie said. "Shall I pick one out—"

"I'm not here for one of your whores, Maisie," he said. "I'm lookin' for Angel and Joey."

"They're upstairs, with Debbie and Lupe. Rooms five and six."

"Anybody else up there?"

"Ginger's got a cowboy with her in room eight. Otherwise everybody's down here."

"Okay," Lane said. "Keep them down here."

"Yes, Sheriff."

Lane went up the stairs. When he got to the top, he took out his gun and checked to make sure it was fully loaded. Then he holstered it and started down the hall.

Joey was crouched between Lupe's spread thighs. His dick was buried in her juicy pussy; as he drove in and out of her, she stared up at the ceiling with a bored look on her face. Many men had taken her this way, with no knowledge of what they were doing. She had picked out the same spot on her ceiling to stare at each time.

"Yeah, yeah," Joey was saying, "you like it, don't you, Mama?"

She said, "Oh, sí, senor, I like it." She wondered why he was calling her "Mama."

"Yeah, yeah . . ." He was moaning when suddenly the door opened. She moved her eyes from that point on the ceiling to look at the man in the doorway. She saw the badge on his chest, and knew there was going to be trouble.

"Senor," she said, pounding on Joey's back, "senor, stop . . ."

"Stop?" Joey asked. "I ain't ever gonna stop—"

"Joey!"

"Wha—" Joey looked over his shoulder, saw the sheriff. "What the hell, Sheriff—"

"Get up," Lane said. "On your feet."

"I'm a little busy here, Sheriff."

"Get off!" Lupe said, pounding on his back. "Let me up!"

She managed to push Joey off her, rolled out of bed, and stood up, not bothering to cover her nudity.

"Get out, Lupe."

"Sí, Senor."

She bent over, her big breasts swaying, picked up her clothes and ran out past the sheriff.

"Jesus, I was just gettin' ready to—"

"Get your gun."

"What?"

"Pick up your gun."

Joey looked at his gun, which was hanging on the bedpost.

"What's goin' on?"

"You tried to rape a woman today," the sheriff said. "That's against the law."

"Wha—Hey, you told us to—"

"I never told you to rape a woman, Joey," Lane said. "Now get dressed, and get your gun."

"Ah . . . you better talk to Angel, Sheriff," Joey said. "He's across the hall."

"Sure," Lane said, "I'll talk to the Angel, after I finish talking to you."

"Okay," Joey said. "I'll get dressed."

But for some reason, before he touched any of his clothes, he reached for his gun and removed the gun belt from the bedpost.

Lane drew and fired twice. Joey danced a bit as each bullet hit him, then fell onto the bed, dead.

The sheriff stepped into the hall and then to the side, still holding his gun. The door to room six opened and Angel came running out, naked, holding his gun.

"Hold it, Angel."

Angel stopped. He looked into room five first, saw Joey on the bed. Then he turned and looked at the sheriff. "What the hell—"

"You two tried to rape a woman," Lane said. "A guest in this town. That's against the law."

"What the hell are you tryin' to pull, Lane?" Angel said.

"Debbie, you in there?" Lane called.

"I-I'm here."

"Come on out, with your clothes."

Debbie came out, holding her clothes.

"Go on downstairs."

"Yes, sir."

She hurried to the steps and ran down.

"Drop the gun, Angel."

"Pendejo," Angel said. "Do you know what the word means?"

"No."

"It has two meanings," Angel said. "Coward is one. Are you a coward? Will you shoot me without giving me a chance?"

"You had your chance, Angel," Lane said. "You and Joey had a simple job to do, and you messed it up."

"It's Adams, isn't it? You fear him."

"I don't fear anybody, Angel," Lane said. "You wanna drop the gun, or you wanna try to make a play?"

"If I drop it, you will kill me," Angel said. "If I try to make a play, you will kill me."

"See?" Lane asked. "You still have a choice, don't you?"

"Dying is not much of a choice, Senor."

"It's the only choice you've got."

Angel shrugged, and made his play. He tried to turn toward the sheriff. But Lane fired twice and Angel fell to the floor.

Lane stepped forward, kicked the gun down the hall. The door to room eight opened and Ginger, a blousy redhead, stuck her head out.

"Can I come out?" she asked.

"Sure, Ginger," he said. "You can come out now. It's all over."

FIFTEEN

Sheriff Lane knocked on the door of Loretta Burns's room.

"W-who is it?"

"It's the sheriff, Miss Burns."

"What do you want?"

"I came to talk to you," he said. "About the two men you say . . . assaulted you."

She opened the door a crack and looked out at him.

"You don't have to be afraid, ma'am," he said. "It's all over."

"What's over?"

"The two men," he said. "They won't bother you anymore."

"You arrested them?"

"They're dead," the sheriff said. "I killed them when they resisted arrest. So you see, you don't have to be afraid."

"I don't?"

"No."

"Well . . . thank you."

"Will you be stayin' in town?" he asked. "Until you find your black chest?"

"Well . . . yes."

"Well," he said, "if I think of anyone who can help you, I'll let you know."

"A-all right," she said. "Please do."

"Ma'am," he said, touching the brim of his hat.

She watched him walk down the hall, and when he disappeared from sight, she went back into her room and closed the door.

She locked it.

Clint saw the sheriff coming out of the hotel. The lawman spotted him and stopped, waiting for him to approach.

"You talk to your deputy?" Clint asked.

"I did," Lane said, "and I just talked to the lady. I told her she doesn't have to worry anymore."

"And why would that be?"

"Angel and Joey are dead."

"Both of them?"

"Both."

"You?"

"They resisted arrest."

"So you tried to arrest them?"

"I did," Lane said. "That's my job, after all."

Clint didn't say anything.

"You look surprised."

"Do I?"

"Yeah," Lane said. "Maybe you heard some things about me you shouldn't have believed. I do my job, Adams."

"Well," Clint said, "looks like you certainly did today. Good job, Sheriff."

He walked past the lawman into the hotel and up to Loretta's room.

"Who is it?" she called when he knocked.

"Clint Adams."

She opened the door a crack, saw that it was him, and then opened it wider.

"Just wanted to check on you—"

"The sheriff was here," she said. "He says he . . . he killed those two men."

"Don't start thinking he did his job," Clint said. "Dead just means they can't testify that he sent them after you."

"That's what I thought," she said, hugging herself as if she was cold.

"Can I come in?"

"Yes" she said, "although I don't know why you would want to after the way I've treated you."

She backed away. He entered and closed the door.

"My guess is you've been pretty unsettled since you got here," he said.

She laughed and said, "That's putting it mildly. I must apologize to you for my actions. And for trying to hire you to kill those two men."

"I understand," he said. "I accept your apology."

"So what happens now?" she asked.

"My guess is, the sheriff will try again. He'll send someone over who's a bit more reputable."

"But still crooked?"

"Oh, yes," Clint said. "You've put up a hundred dollars—"

"I was going to pay those two men a hundred and fifty."

"—so the sheriff figures you have a lot more money than that. Plus, if you're so anxious to get that chest back, there might be something of value in it."

She didn't reply.

"Is there?"

"No answer.

"Okay, it's none of my business," he said. "Just do me a favor. Be more careful about who you hire next time."

"I will."

"Good luck," he said, and left.

SIXTEEN

Sheriff Lane went back to his office. As he opened the door, he thought he saw the deputy jump up from his desk, but he decided to let it go.

"What happened, Sheriff?"

"Angel and Joey are dead."

"Huh?"

"They resisted arrest," Lane said, sitting behind his desk. Was the chair warm? "You remember that, okay?"

"Resisted arrest," Deputy Simons said. "I got it. Where are they?"

"At the undertaker's," Lane said. "Next stop, potter's field."

"Okay. Uh, what about Clint Adams and the, uh, the lady?" the deputy asked.

"What about them?"

"Well, is she satisfied?"

"The men who tried to rape her are dead," Lane said. "Why wouldn't she be satisfied?"

But Loretta Burns was not satisfied.

Maybe the men who had attacked her were dead, but if

Clint Adams was right, and they were sent by the sheriff, then there was still danger. If the sheriff wanted her money, and her chest, how was she supposed to keep him from taking them?

Also, there was Randolph.

When Randolph realized she was gone, and with the chest, he would look for her, and when he found her, he'd kill her himself. He wouldn't send anybody else to do it. Randolph was the type who liked to do things himself.

She thought she'd be safe among the simpletons in the West. Now she realized she was wrong. She needed somebody to help her navigate her way through these murky waters. Somebody who could handle the sheriff, and Randolph, if it came to that.

That person was Clint Adams, the professional gunman.

And she had let him walk out of her room after bidding her, "Good luck."

She changed her clothes, donned a shawl she thought might make her less desirable to these Western morons, and went to find him.

SEVENTEEN

Clint went to the Golden Palace for a beer before heading back to his room to collect his gear. He was going to ride out of town tonight, get a few miles under his belt, and then camp for the night. That was better than spending one more night in this town, where the sheriff was crazy and there was no telling what he would do. The last thing he needed was to have to shoot a lawman. Even a crazy one.

When he entered the saloon, there were a few men there who had also been there when he pulled Loretta Burns away from Angel and Joey. They stared at him as he went to the bar and ordered a beer.

The bartender was also the same one from that afternoon.

"You're back," the bartender said.

"Yeah."

"Did you, uh, have trouble with Angel and Joey?" he asked.

"I didn't," Clint said. "The sheriff took care of them. At least, that's what I heard."

"Oh, yeah," the bartender said. "I heard they was dead, but I thought you—"

"Nope, not me," Clint said. "I'll have a beer."

"Comin' up."

He brought over a frothy beer and set it in front of Clint. He lifted it to his mouth and was about to drink when he saw, in the mirror, Loretta Burns enter the saloon. Actually, first she stuck her head in, and when she saw him, she came in the rest of the way.

"Aw no," the bartender said. "Is she gonna be trouble again?"

"She wasn't the trouble the last time," Clint said. "That was Angel and Joey. Remember?"

"Yeah, yeah," the bartender said, "but do me a favor and get her out of here."

Clint picked up his beer, turned, and walked toward Loretta.

"Hey," she said. "I was looking for—Hey!"

He grabbed her arm and took her through the batwing doors, outside with him. There he released her and sipped his beer.

"What are you doing?" he asked.

"I was trying to tell you, I was looking for you."

"Don't go walking into saloons alone, Loretta."

"I wasn't alone," she said. "You were there."

"What do you want?"

"I want to hire you."

"We talked about this already."

"No, no," she said, "not to kill somebody. I want to hire you to find that chest for me. My black box."

"I can't do that."

"Why not?"

"I'm leaving town tomorrow," he said. "In fact, I was going to leave tonight."

"Which way are you going?" she asked.

In fact, he was going west, but he knew what would happen if he told her that.

"You're going west, aren't you?" she asked.

He hesitated, then said, "Yes."

"So then you can look," she said. "No harm done."

"Loretta—"

"I'll pay you."

"I don't want—"

"A thousand dollars."

He hesitated, again. Took another swallow of beer.

"Can I have some of that?"

He looked at her, then shrugged and held the glass out to her. She took a sip and passed it back. Two old maids walked past and sniffed at the both of them.

"God, I hate women like that," she said.

"What's so important about this chest?"

"It's mine," she said. "It belongs to me. I'm lodging a complaint with the stage company. So in a way, you'd be taking their money."

"Well," he said, "that's okay, then, isn't it?"

"Yes, it is."

"If I was to find the chest, I would need a buckboard to bring it in, right?"

"Right. I would pay for that. First, though, you could ride out and find it. You have a horse, right?"

"I have a very good horse."

"Then it probably wouldn't take you long."

"It depends on how far away from here you were when the chest fell off the stage. I'd have to go back to the first stage station and see if they saw the chest. If not, then I have to keep going."

"At that point, I'll add another thousand dollars," she said.

He stared at her.

"That's two thousand."

"I can add."

"I wasn't inferring you couldn't."

She took his beer and sipped it again, then passed it back. At this point she almost seemed human.

"I'll think about it," he said, and stepped onto the boardwalk.

"What about your beer?"

"You finish it."

He started to walk away.

"Hey."

He turned.

"Does this mean you're not leaving tonight?"

"That's right," he said. "I'll leave in the morning."

"Are you going back to the hotel?"

"Yes."

She put the beer glass down on the walk and hurried after him. "Can I walk with you?"

"Come on."

He started walking, and she had to run to catch up.

EIGHTEEN

In the morning Clint rose, sat on the edge of the bed and shook his head. He was going to do it. Not because she was beautiful, not because of the two thousand dollars. But because he was curious.

What the hell was in that box?

Before going to their respective rooms the night before, they had agreed to meet for breakfast in the morning. She was already sitting at a table in the hotel dining room when he got there. It was sufficiently far enough away from the door and windows that he did not have a complaint.

"Well?"

"Steak and eggs is good."

"No, I mean—"

"I know what you mean." He sat down, poured himself some coffee from the pot on the table. The waiter came over.

"Steak and eggs," he said. "Two."

"Comin' up."

As he walked away, Loretta leaned forward and asked, "So?"

"I'll do it."

She sat back, smiled.

"Thank you."

"Sure." He drank some coffee. "You should do that more often."

"What's that?"

"Smile."

The smile dropped away.

"I haven't had much to smile about in a long time."

"That what you're running away from?" he asked.

"What?"

He shrugged.

"Bad marriage?"

"The worst."

"How bad?"

"Bad enough for me to swear off men."

"Ooh" he said, "that's pretty bad."

"Yes," she said, "it is."

They didn't talk much over breakfast. Apparently, he'd gotten everything out of her that he was going to.

"Good?" he asked, trying at one point.

"Very good," she said. "Thank you."

After a few minutes she put her knife and fork down and stared at him.

"You want to ask me more questions, don't you?"

"Well, yeah . . ."

"Fine," she said. "If you ask me some, I get to ask you some."

"Like what?"

"How many men have you killed?" she asked. "What does it feel like to kill a man? Do you like—"

He held up his hand to stop her.

"Point taken," he said. "Let's just eat in peace."

She picked up her knife and fork. "Fine with me."

They both shut their mouths and tucked in.

After he paid the bill, they walked out to the lobby.

"Will you be staying here?" he asked. "In the hotel?"

"Yes. You'll find me here when you come back."

"How long will you stay?"

"Until you get back."

"And you'll be okay?"

She smiled slightly. "I'll stay away from the sheriff, and strange men," she said.

"Do you have a gun?"

"I did," she said.

He looked at her.

"It's in my trunk."

"One more reason to get it back, then," he said.

"Yes."

"Well . . . I have to check out, and pay my bill," he said.

"I have some shopping to do," she said. "Do you want some money now? For expenses?"

"No," he said. "When I get back will be fine."

"Be still my beating heart," she said. "An honest man?"

"There are a few of us around."

"If we're not careful, Mr. Adams," she said, "you may improve my opinion of men."

"Well," he said, "I'll do my best, Miss Burns."

She turned and walked out of the hotel. He walked over to the desk.

NINETEEN

Clint went to the livery and had Harley saddle Eclipse. The liveryman walked the horse out of the stable.

"I'm gonna miss this big fella," he said, handing the reins over to Clint. "He listens to me when I talk."

"He does that to you, too?" Clint asked, mounting up.

"You take care of him, now."

"We usually take care of each other," Clint said.

"Well," Harley said, "I get the feeling he takes better care of you than you do him."

Clint stared at Harley for a moment, then said, "You're probably right about that, Harley."

"You ever get back this way, you stop in and see old Harley," the man said.

"I will."

Harley looked up at him and said, "I was talking to the horse."

"Ah," Clint said.

He rode out of Westbrook, wondering if he'd ever locate Loretta Burns's black chest. Even if he did, he wouldn't have any reason to return to town. He could simply send her a telegram. Then—if honesty was so important to her—she could wire him the money she promised to pay him.

If she didn't, he wouldn't have lost anything—except maybe respect for women like Loretta Burns.

Sheriff Lane watched as Clint Adams rode out of town. He'd seen Clint and the Burns woman having breakfast together, and the outcome wasn't hard to figure. In fact, maybe she'd fucked him last night to get him to go along, but Lane was convinced that Clint Adams was going out to look for that chest.

As Clint disappeared from view down the street, Lane crossed the street and entered the telegraph office.

It wasn't a difficult thing to backtrack the stage route. After all, they stuck to the main road. If the box had fallen off the back of the stage and landed in the roads, though, somebody would have found it by now. He kept his eyes peeled for any kind of rutted marks in the ground. If it was as big and heavy as she said, it would have had to be dragged off the road.

He rode for half a day, and his progress was slow. He'd stop from time to time to take a look off the road—in a dry wash or a gulley—to see if he'd find the box, or remnants of it. Anyone who had already found it might not have taken the entire box away with them. They could easily have broken it open and taken anything of value. That would mean they'd leave behind broken pieces. But by the time he reined Eclipse in for some water and beef jerky, he hadn't found anything.

Eclipse was moving fine, showing signs of being his old self. This horse had more stamina than he any other he had ever rode, except maybe for the big black gelding Duke.

The two horses were very close in size and condition, but Duke could go for days and never show sign of strain. The gelding was definitely the most remarkable animal Clint had ever ridden, but Eclipse was a close second.

He refilled his canteen, mounted up, and started off again.

He rode for the second half of the day, found nothing. It would probably take him most of the next day to get to the stage stop. He might have made it today if he'd simply ridden straight there, but he was studying the ground for signs. He wasn't the best tracker in the world, and to look for signs he had to ride slowly. Of course, it might have been smarter to ride directly to the station. If the station manager told him the chest was not on the stage when they stopped, he'd know he'd wasted some time. Of course, if the man told him the chest was there, he'd have to back-track again, figuring he'd missed it somewhere between the station and town.

He passed some side roads to other towns, but didn't see the benefit of stopping. He continued to ride until it started to get dark, and then camped for the night.

He built a fire, put on a pot of coffee, and had a supper of beef jerky. He was traveling light so there'd be no need for a pack horse.

He was pouring himself another cup of trail coffee when he heard a sound. The snapping of a twig beneath some-body's feet. And then a lot of snapping. It was probably the rider who had been following him all day. He figured maybe the sheriff had sent somebody after him, maybe to tail him until he found the box.

He stood up and drew his gun.

"You're not being very quiet," he called out. "Come into the light."

There was some more snapping, some muttered curses, and then a person came lunging out of the brush, almost losing her balance and falling.

Loretta Burns, looking much the worse for wear.

TWENTY

She was wearing riding clothes, but the shirt looked torn and dirty, her hat was hanging down her back, and her hair was a mess, with leaves and branches in it.

"Goddamnit!" she said, then stood up straight and stared at him.

"You lost?" he asked.

"I thought I was."

"Where's your horse?"

"I left it . . . back there," she said, waving. "Do you have any food? I haven't eaten all day."

"When I left you, you said you were going shopping," he said.

"I did," she said. "I bought some riding clothes, and a horse."

"So it's you who's been following me all day?"

"You knew?"

"Of course I knew," he said. "I just didn't know who it was."

"Then why didn't you just let me catch up with you? And eat with you?"

"I thought you might have been a man the sheriff sent after me."

"Well, I'm not," she said. "How about that food?"

"All I have is coffee and beef jerky."

"Anything would be good right about now."

"Fine," he said, holstering his gun. "Have some and I'll go and get your horse."

"Thank you."

As she hunkered down by the fire and poured herself some coffee, he started back through the brush. Eventually he found her horse, a mare tied loosely to a tree. A couple more pulls and the animal would have gotten away.

He walked it back to camp, where she was scarfing down a piece of beef jerky, chewing and washing it down with coffee.

"Take it easy," he said. "That has to last us."

"Why didn't you bring something else?" she asked. "Don't you cowboy types travel with things like beans and bacon?"

"I am not a cowboy," he said, tying her horse off next to Eclipse, and removing the saddle. "You'll have to brush her down."

"Why?"

"If she's going to be fresh in the morning, you'll have to rub her down, brush her, and feed her."

"I usually have someone who does that for me," she said.

"Well," Clint said, "that's not what I'm here for."

"I'm paying you."

"To find your box," he reminded her. "And by the way, while you stayed in town."

"I never said that," she said. "I never said I'd stay in town."

"You said you'd stay at the hotel."

"I said I'd be *registered* at the hotel."

"Okay," he said, "never mind." He squatted by the fire and poured a fresh cup of coffee. She had taken his cup, so he took out the extra. "You better get to your horse."

"Really?"

"Yes, really," he said. "You'll want her to be fresh when you head back to town."

She stood up, but protested, "I'm not going back to town."

"Where are you going, then?"

"With you."

She walked to the horse and started to run her down with her hands.

"No," he said, "like this."

He got up, started to show her how, and then simply did it for her.

It was just easier.

TWENTY-ONE

After the mare was rubbed down and fed, they sat around the fire and argued some more.

"I can't go back to town," she told him.

"Why not?"

"I'm frightened all the time," she said. "It's not a feeling I like."

"Well, I don't blame you," he said. "There's a lot to be afraid of, if you don't know what you're doing."

"Then you know why I can't stay," she said. "I would surely be robbed, and raped."

Clint frowned. What she was saying was probably true. He probably should never have left her behind.

"You weren't afraid to go after me."

"Yes, I was," she said, "but I had to do it, anyway. I'm not used to being a coward, Mr. Adams."

"If we're going to ride together," he said, "you're going to have to start calling me Clint."

"Then we are going to ride together?" she asked. "You'll let me come?"

"Yes," he said. "Yes, you can come. But you have to do everything I tell you."

"I will."

"If you don't," he said, "I swear I'll drop you at the next town—and it won't be as civilized as Westbrook."

She looked up from her coffee and said, "Westbrook was civilized?"

In the morning, she rolled out of the bedroll with a loud moan. "Oh my God," she said. "My back."

"Get up and stretch it out," he said. "And then come have some coffee. We have to get moving."

"What's the rush?" she asked. "The chest isn't going anywhere."

"Unless someone else has found it already."

She was stretching and stopped to stare at him. "What?"

"You didn't think of that?"

She came to the fire and accepted a cup of coffee from him.

"Actually, no," she said, "but I can see how foolish I was. Of course someone else could have found it. What will we do then?"

"We'll cross that bridge when we come to it," he said.

She nodded.

"Tell me, could falling off the back of the stage have caused it to fall apart?"

"No," she said. "It's too well constructed."

"So it'll just sit there until somebody finds it."

"Until *we* find it," she clarified.

"Depending on how fast the stage was going when it fell off," Clint said, "it might or might not roll."

"Roll?"

"End over end," Clint said, demonstrating with his hands. "If it falls and lands flat, it might sit right in the road.

But if it rolls—or tumbles—it could end up off the road."

"By the side of the road?"

"Unless there's a hill, a gulley, or a dry wash for it to roll down."

"Then how do we find it?"

He stood up and poured the remnants of the coffee on the fire to douse it.

"We look, Loretta," he said. "And we look very carefully."

TWENTY-TWO

Clint made Loretta saddle her own horse, showed her how to make sure it was cinched in tight. Then they saddled up and rode out.

"You have to stay behind me," he said.

"Why?"

"If you ride ahead of me, you'll trample any sign I might find," he explained.

"Why can't I ride next to you?"

"Because you'll talk to me," he said. "Distract me from what I'm doing."

"I won't talk to you," she said. "I promise."

"You'll still distract me," he said.

"Why?"

He looked at her. "Because you're beautiful."

He swore she blushed, then turned her head away. Finally, she dropped back to ride behind him.

Clint smiled and led the way.

Back in Westbrook Sheriff Lane had gotten an immediate reply to the telegram he'd sent the day Clint left.

ON MY WAY it read, signed "Duffy."

Duffy showed up the next day, since he had only been a couple of towns away.

As he entered the sheriff's office, Lane looked up, then looked over at Deputy Simons.

"Simons, go make some rounds."

"I already made my morning rounds, Sheriff—"

"Then make your afternoon rounds early," Lane said. "Go!"

Simons left, looking Duffy up and down as he went. Duffy ignored him and sat down.

"Coffee?"

"Just tell me why I'm here?"

Duffy stretched out his long legs, folded his hands in his lap and stared at the sheriff. He was thirty-three years old, and all he knew how to do was kill. It was a talent that had come to him naturally, which was odd because his parents were Quakers. Israel Duffy was the only Quaker killer Sheriff Lane had ever met.

"You want to make a thousand dollars?"

"You want me to burn down the town?"

"I want you to track one man and one woman," Lane said, "and kill 'em."

"When?" Duffy never even asked "Why?" It was none of his business.

"Now. They left here yesterday."

"When do I get paid?"

"When you kill the woman," Lane said. "She has the money on her."

Lane had gone through the woman's room during the day and found no money, but he was sure she had the thousand on her.

What he wanted was the box.

"And what do you get for this?" Duffy asked. "Do I bring anything back to you?"

"Yes," Lane said, "a black chest."

"Chest. What kinda chest?"

"The kind a woman packs with clothes."

"You want the woman's clothes?"

"I want whatever's in the box, Duffy," Lane said. "In fact, you don't even have to open it. Just bring it back here."

"I'll need a packhorse or a buckboard."

"So?"

"I ain't buyin' it with my own money."

Lane sighed, opened his bottom drawer, used a key to open a metal box, took out some cash, and locked the box back up.

He reached across the desk. Duffy extended one of his long arms and accepted the money.

"They'll be movin' slow," Lane said, "so you shouldn't have much trouble catchin' up."

"What's the woman's name?"

"Burns," Lane said, "Loretta Burns."

"She anybody?"

"No," Lane said. "She came to town on the stage, only her black chest had fallen off along the way. She was tryin' to hire somebody to go out and find it, for a hundred dollars."

"A hundred?" Duffy asked. "Where's the thousand come in?"

"She's carryin' it on her. I haven't seen it, but somebody I know did."

"Okay," Duffy said. He stood up. "So who's the man?"

Lane hesitated, then said, "His name is Clint Adams."

Duffy stopped short. "The Gunsmith?"

Lane smiled.

"What do you want done with him?"

"He's yours," Lane said. "He's in my way, so whatever you want to do, you do it. My preference is to have him dead so he don't come back here. How you do it is up to you."

Duffy looked down at the money in his hand, suddenly aware that it was more than he expected.

"Yeah," Lane said, "you might want to get yourself some help."

"I don't need help," Duffy said, "but I'll take along some backup."

"You do that," Lane said.

TWENTY-THREE

Loretta remained mounted while Clint stepped down to study the ground.

"What is it?" she asked.

"Something was dragged here," he said, "but I can't tell what."

"Dragged how far?"

"Well, to the end of the road, here," Clint said, walking. "Then it must have been lifted up onto a wagon. There are several wheel ruts here, but that's normal this close to a town."

"What town?"

"That signpost we passed a mile or so back said Bolden, Arizona."

"Do you know it?"

"No," he said, mounting up, "never been there, never heard of it."

"But we're going?"

He nodded and said, "We're going, just to see what's what."

* * *

They rode into Bolden side by side. The street was filled with ruts from buckboard and wagons, possibly even a stage or two, if this was a stage stop.

Clint had told Loretta to let him do the talking. Not to say one word, unless he asked her to.

He thought she was going to protest, but in the end she just nodded her head and said, "All right."

But since they weren't yet around other people, she asked, "What are we going to do first?"

"Talk to the sheriff."

"You're going to trust the sheriff?" she asked. "After what we went through in Westbrook?"

"Not all sheriffs are crooked, Loretta," he said. "I'm going to talk to the local lawman and try to figure him out. Once I have we'll tell him why we're here and see if he can help us."

She just shook her head and rode along with him. When he spotted the sheriff's office he pointed Eclipse that way. Loretta followed.

If he didn't have Loretta with him he probably would have gone into a saloon to talk with a bartender first. They usually give him the straight story on the local lawman. But he wasn't about to take Loretta into a saloon again. They'd had enough trouble with that.

They dismounted and tied off their horses. When they mounted the boardwalk, Clint stopped in front of the door and said to her, "Remember, don't talk."

"What if he asks me a question?"

"Then answer it as briefly as possible."

She nodded, and he opened the door.

Duffy picked up Clint Adams's trail quickly, tracked him until he camped and was joined by another rider. Had to be the woman.

As Lane had promised, they were moving slowly, probably because they were watching for any sign of the box along the way. Duffy knew he wasn't going to be able to make a move on them until they found the box. He didn't want to kill them, and then have to go and find the box himself. Leave that up to them.

He was a few miles from the place where he'd agreed to meet his backup, Dennis Franks. Franks was a reliable gun who worked fairly cheap. He would adequately watch Duffy's back.

Duffy had become one of those men curious about what was in that box.

TWENTY-FOUR

"Sheriff?" Clint asked, as they entered the office.

The Sheriff of Bolden, Arizona looked around from what he had been doing and stared at the two of them. His eyes were drawn to Loretta's beauty.

"Hello," he said. He was a young man, in his early thirties. At first Clint thought he was a deputy, but then the man turned and Clint saw the sheriff's badge.

He had been cleaning a rifle, which he now set aside.

"I'm Sheriff Ryker. Can I help you?"

"Sheriff, my name is Clint Adams. This is Miss Loretta Burns."

"Adams?" Ryker asked. "The Gunsmith, you mean?"

"That's right."

Suddenly, Clint became more interesting to him than Loretta. "Well," he said, "what's the Gunsmith doing in Bolden, Arizona?"

"We're passing through," Clint said. "I usually check in with the local law when I ride into a town."

"I appreciate that, Mr. Adams," Ryker said. "And the lady?"

"She's traveling with me," Clint said.

"Will you be stayin' in Bolden?"

"One night," Clint said. "Then we'll move on."

"Then maybe we could get a drink together?" Ryker asked.

"I'm sorry, Sheriff," Loretta said, "but I don't think that would be—"

"I'm sorry, ma'am," Ryker said, "but I was talking to the Gunsmith."

Looking embarrassed, Loretta said, "I see."

"I don't see why we can't do that, Sheriff," Clint said.

"Good. The saloon across the street? In one hour? That'll give you time to see to your horses and get, uh, rooms at the hotel."

"Okay," Clint said. "I'll see you in an hour."

"Nice to meet you, ma'am," Ryker said.

Loretta only nodded, and she and Clint left the office.

Outside on the boardwalk in front of the office she said, "He's very impressed with you. Why didn't you ask him?"

"Because I didn't get a read on him," Clint said. "He's too impressed. I'll be able to figure him out over a drink."

"And what am I supposed to do while you and the sheriff are having a drink?" she asked.

"Stay in your room," he said.

"And do what?"

"Rest," he said. "We'll be leaving again in the morning. With or without your black chest."

"But why can't I walk around—"

"Have you already forgotten what happened when you walked around Westbrook?"

She looked away. "No."

"Then we'll get a couple of rooms, and you will stay in yours until I come and get you."

"Can we eat then?"

"Yes," he said. "Then we'll eat."

"Okay."

They stepped down and mounted their horses.

They left their horses in the livery, stopped at one of Bolden's two hotels, and checked into a couple of rooms.

"This is . . . filthy," she said, looking around. They had left his gear in his room, and were now in hers. They were identical.

"It's filthy only by comparison with where you usually stay," he said. "It's fine."

"If you say so."

"How was your room in Westbrook?"

"Better than this, I suppose."

"Why do you only suppose?"

"I—I guess I was too angry the whole time I was there to notice."

"Staying here won't hurt you, Loretta."

"I know it."

"I'm going to have that drink with the sheriff, now," he said. "By the time I come back, I should know something helpful."

"I hope so."

"I know so," he said. "Just get some rest."

She nodded and said, "Okay."

He opened her door and started out.

"Clint?"

"Yes?"

"Be careful."

He smiled. "I will."

TWENTY-FIVE

As Clint walked into the hotel across from the sheriff's office, he saw Sheriff Ryker standing at the bar. It was midday, and there weren't very many other patrons in the place. It was a small place, no gaming tables, just whiskey and beer.

"There you are," Ryker said. "Beer?"

"Yes."

"Comin' up."

Ryker signaled to the bartender, who brought over two beers. From the way the barman looked at him Clint felt that the Sheriff had not revealed his identify.

"Thank you," Clint said.

"I don't mind telling you," Ryker said, "I'm impressed."

"With what?"

"Your presence."

"Not my reputation?"

"Reputations can be inflated," Ryker said. "This is my opportunity to find out just how much. Do you mind answering questions?"

Normally, Clint did mind. But answering the sheriff's questions would help him evaluate the man.

"No," he said, "go ahead and ask."

Duffy met up with Dennis Franks at the appointed place and shared a bottle of whiskey the man had.

"The Gunsmith, huh?" Franks asked.

"That's right."

"You gonna try to take him, face to face?"

"I don't know yet," Duffy asked. "First I've got to find that box."

"What's in it?"

"I don't know," Duffy said, "but it must be something worth more than five hundred dollars."

He had told Franks that the woman was carrying five hundred dollars, not a thousand. And he promised to pay the man a hundred.

"Can we open it when we find it?" Franks asked. "Take a peek?"

"I don't know," Duffy said, passing the bottle back. "I'm thinkin' about that, too."

Ryker's questions were the normal kind. Plenty of reporters had asked Clint the same question—when had he realized he was good with a gun, when did he kill his first man, did he know Bat Masterson and Wild Bill Hickok?—as well as many, many young men. Ryker was completely forgetting he a lawman and was just in awe.

Clint was convinced that this young man was clean as the driven snow. But still, he had some questions of his own.

"So, when did you become a lawman?" he asked.

"Oh, not long ago," Ryker said. "This is my first badge. Our sheriff got killed and nobody wanted the job, so I stepped up."

"When is the next election?"

"Next month, as a matter of fact."

"You going to run?"

"Yes," Ryker said, "I like this job. I want to try to keep it."

"Do you usually know when strangers come into town?"

"Yes," Ryker said. "If you hadn't come to me, the clerk at the hotel would have told me about you."

"That's good."

"The bartenders know to contact me, too."

They were sitting at a table, working on their second beers.

"Did you tell this bartender who I am?"

"No," Ryker said.

"Why not?"

"I didn't think he needed to know."

Clint sat back, regarded the young man for a moment, then decided to go ahead and open up.

"Sheriff," he said. "Miss Burns and I are not really just passing through."

"Oh?" Ryker's face lit up with curiosity, but then he frowned. "You're not here to kill anyone, are you? Because I'd have to try to stop you. And that wouldn't be good for the rest of my career."

"Why not?"

"Because you'd probably kill me."

"And knowing that, you'd still try to stop me?"

"Yes, sir."

"Why?"

"It's my job."

"You're a good man, Ryker."

"Thank you, sir. So, are you? Here to kill somebody, I mean?"

"No," Clint said. "I'm not here to kill somebody. We're here looking for an object."

"What kind of object?"

"It's a chest," Clint said, "a big black box."

"What's in it?"

"Some of Miss Burns's possessions," Clint said, "like clothes, and family, uh, items." He almost said "heirlooms," but that would have made it sound valuable.

"So what makes you think it's here?"

"I don't know if it is," Clint said. "It fell off the back of the stage she took to Westbrook, so we've been backtracking the route. Outside of town we found a spot on the road that looks like something was dragged a few feet, and then possibly lifted—like put on a buckboard."

"Hmm," Ryker said. "Let me give it some thought, and maybe I can come up with something. Have you eaten?"

"Not for a while," Clint said. "I thought I'd go back to the hotel and get Miss Burns and take her for something."

"The only good place in town to eat is called Dave's Café. Down the street. Good steaks."

"Thanks," Clint said. "I'll take her there."

"And if I find out anything, I'll let you know."

"Okay," Clint said, standing up. "Thanks for the beers."

"Anytime, Mr. Adams. Anytime."

TWENTY-SIX

Clint knocked on Loretta's door. She answered it immediately, and rushed into his arms. He was very aware of her full breasts pressing against his chest.

"What's going on?" he asked.

"I'm glad to see you, that's all," she said. "I—I've been afraid every time I heard footsteps in the hall." Abruptly, she pushed him away from her and backed up, folding her arms. "I hate this place. I hate being like this."

"You hate the hotel, or the town?"

"I hate your Wild West," she said. "You can keep it. As soon as I have my property back, I'm heading east."

"Well, before you do that, would you like to go out and have a steak?"

"Yes!" she said, her eyes widening. "Can we go now?"

"Yes," he said. "Right now. The sheriff told me about a café that has good steaks."

"Then let's go!" she said.

Duffy and Franks came to the place in the road Clint and Loretta had found the drag marks.

"Yeah," Duffy said, "somethin' was dragged here."

"The box?"

"Maybe."

"Maybe somebody found it and took it into that town up ahead. Bolden."

"And maybe," Duffy said, "Adams and the woman went there."

"So we go there, too?" Franks said.

Duffy mounted up and said, "We go there."

At Dave's, they ordered two steak dinners and, while eating, Clint told her about his conversation with the sheriff.

"Wow, he's in awe of you."

"I suppose."

"Does that happen to you a lot?"

"Sometimes?"

"With women, too?"

"Sometimes."

"I'm sorry I didn't know who you were when we met," she said.

"Why should you?"

"Well, you're famous," she said. "Maybe if I hadn't been so angry—"

"Do you know who I am now?"

"Well, because you told me, but . . . I still never heard of you before."

"I'm sure there are a lot of people who haven't heard of me," he said.

"Does that bother you?"

"No, why should it?"

"I don't know," she said. "I just thought men with reputations liked it when people knew who they were. I mean, isn't that the point of having a reputation?"

"I guess I don't really know the point of having a reputation, then," he said. "See, I just . . . have one. I never went looking for it."

"So you don't like having a reputation?"

"Not very much, no."

"Then why don't you . . . stop?"

He laughed. "Can you tell me how to do that?"

"Take off your guns and get a regular job."

"If I did that," Clint said, "I'd be dead in a week."

She paused in her chewing and asked, "Why?"

"As soon as some young gun heard I wasn't wearing my gun, they'd come looking for me," Clint said. "Unarmed, I'd be dead."

"So, you have to live like this, whether you like it or not?"

"That's right."

"That's terrible."

"Eat your steak," he said. "I'm used to it, after all these years."

Over dessert she said to him, "I'm sorry."

"About what?"

"About being a bitch," she said. "I mean, from the moment we met."

"You were having a hard time."

"No reason to take it out on you," she said. "It sounds like you've been having a hard time a lot longer than I have."

"Ah," he said, "you're feeling sorry for me."

"Well, yeah, I probably am," she said. "I can't imagine living the way you live."

"Well," he said, "you'll never have to. Be thankful for that—and eat your pie."

TWENTY-SEVEN

After they finished, they stepped outside the café.

"I guess you've been to a lot of towns like this over the years," she said.

"Like this, like Westbrook, like Dodge City," he said. "Yeah, a lot of towns."

"Wouldn't you like to . . . settle down?"

"No," he said. "Settling down's not for me. I'll just keep moving . . ."

"Until."

"What?"

"It sounded like there was an 'until' there," she said.

"Until I meet a faster gun," Clint said.

"And then what?"

"And then he'll kill me."

"That's the way you expect to die?"

"That seems like the only way my life could end," he said.

"But . . . that's so sad."

"Maybe it is," he said. "But I'd rather die like that than in bed, wasting away." He was thinking of Doc Holliday.

She was about to say something but instead broke off and said, "Is that the sheriff coming at us?"

"It sure is. Looks like he has something on his mind."

They waited for the man to reach them.

Duffy and Franks reined their horses in just outside of town.

"What?" Franks asked.

"Two strangers riding into town together will attract attention."

"So we'll ride in separate."

"No," Duffy said. "Two strangers riding in that way would attract attention, also. Especially if Adams and the woman have already ridden in."

"So what do we do?"

"It's what *you* do," Duffy said. "You ride in and find out if Adams is there."

"How do I find that out?"

"Hey," Duffy said, "if the Gunsmith is in a small town like Bolden, you'll hear about it. Just have a drink."

"And a whore?"

"Whatever," Duffy said.

"I'll need some money."

Duffy passed him some.

"A couple of drinks, and one whore," he said, warningly. "You're there to get information about Adams, or about the box, not to have a good time."

"I'll see if I can do both," Franks said.

"How was the food?" Ryker asked.

"As good as you said," Clint said. "What's on your mind?"

"I've got something to show you," the lawman said. "You want to come with me?"

"Sure."

They both stepped down from the boardwalk.

"Both of you?" Ryker asked.

"Why not?" Clint asked. "If it's about the chest, Miss Burns has a right to know."

"I suppose," the sheriff said with a shrug. "Okay, then, this way."

TWENTY-EIGHT

Clint became concerned as they approached the undertaker's office.

"Maybe you should stay outside," he said to Loretta.

"Why? Are we going to see a body?" she asked the sheriff.

"Not really," he said. "But it is an undertaker's office. I can't guarantee there isn't a body lying around."

"I've seen bodies before," Loretta said. "Let's just go in and see what the sheriff has to show us."

"Okay," Clint said. "Let's go."

Sheriff Ryker led the way into the office.

"Eddie!" he shouted.

A man came through a curtained doorway from a back room. He was in his forties, looked more like an accountant than an undertaker.

"My God, but you're beautiful!" he said to Loretta.

"Well . . . thank you."

"This is Eddie Dowd. He's the town's new undertaker."

"The old one died," Dowd said with a shrug. "He was my first customer."

"Eddie, these folks think something was brought into

town from the road, something that had to be dragged, and then transported by wagon."

"Oh," he said, "that."

"What was it?" Clint asked.

Eddie Dowd looked embarrassed.

"I was driving my rig back to town and the coffin I was transporting . . . fell off."

"Oh," Loretta said.

"I was alone, so I had to drag it to the wagon and put it back in. It wasn't easy, but—"

"That's enough, Eddie," Ryker said. "You can go back to work now."

Dowd shrugged, said, "Ma'am," to Loretta, and then back through the curtained doorway.

"When we talked earlier, I forgot that Eddie told me this story yesterday," Ryker said to Clint. He looked at Loretta. "I'm sorry it's not what you were looking for, ma'am."

"Thank you," she said.

"Guess you folks better get some rest and then start out again in the morning."

"We'll do that, Sheriff."

They went back to the hotel. Along the way, Clint saw a rider come into town and rein in his horse in front of the saloon. He appeared not to be from around those parts. What were the odds, he thought, of three strangers coming to town on the same day?

"What is it?" Loretta asked.

"Nothing," Clint said. "I just saw somebody."

"Somebody you know?"

"No," he said, "that's the problem. Somebody I don't know."

He walked her to her room and then told her he'd be back.

"Wait!" She grabbed his arm. "Where are you going?"

"The saloon."

"Now?" she asked. "You want a drink *now?*"

"I want to go over to the saloon," he said. "It's got nothing to do with getting a drink."

"Well, make sure you come back," she said.

"I will."

"No, I mean come back here," she said. "To my room."

"I'll be back, Loretta," he said. "Don't worry. You can see the saloon from your window. Watch me walk over there."

"Good idea," she said. "I'm going to do that."

He left her room, closing the door behind him. She was already at the window.

Down on the street, he looked up and saw her standing at the window. She was starting to get more and more frightened, and clingy. He knew it had been a bad idea for her to come along.

He crossed the street, stopped at the stranger's horse. The animal was wet, had been ridden a long way, and quickly. Somebody leaving Westbrook and riding hard could make up a one-day lag on Clint and Loretta.

But there was no point in sending someone after them to kill them. Most likely, the sheriff would send someone to trail them, wait for them to find the chest, and then take it away from them.

However, Clint did not think the sheriff would send a single man to do that. This one had probably ridden in to do some scouting.

Clint decided to go into the saloon and give the man something to scout.

TWENTY-NINE

Clint entered the saloon, which, even at this late hour in the day, was almost empty. He looked around, saw a couple of men seated at tables, and the stranger standing at the bar.

"Got a whorehouse in town?" the man was asking.

"Nope," the bartender said.

"What? How can a town not have a cathouse?"

Clint walked to the bar, gave the man a wide berth, and ordered a beer.

"You know where I can get a whore, then?" the man asked.

"Next town," the bartender said. "Called Denbow. They've got a whore."

"One whore?"

"One whore."

"What the hell is goin' on around here?" the man demanded, looking around.

The two seated men ignored him, one working on a beer, the other a bottle of whiskey. So the man looked at Clint.

"You believe this? No whores?"

"I believe it," Clint said. "It's a nice little town."

"How can it be a nice town when a man can't get his ashes hauled?"

"Guess you'll just have to content yourself with drinking," Clint said.

"You been in town long?" the man asked.

"Yep," Clint said. "Most of the day, in fact."

He saw a wary look come into the man's eyes.

"Just got to town today?"

"That's right."

"I, uh, just got here, myself."

"I know," Clint said. "I saw you ride in."

"Mmm," the man said, turning back toward the bar. He started working on his beer, studiously avoiding Clint's eyes.

"What brings you to town?" Clint asked.

"Oh, uh, just passin' through."

"Lookin' for a whore?"

"Among other things," he said. "A whore, a beer, you know."

"What's your name?"

"Name?"

"Yeah," Clint said. "I'm Clint Adams."

"My name's, uh, Franks."

"You're Clint Adams?" the bartender asked. "The Gunsmith?"

"That's right."

"Wow," the barman said. "Whaddaya think of that?" He was looking at Franks.

"Um, yeah, what about it?" Franks said. "A famous man. Well, thanks for the beer. I'll, uh, head for that other town to find that whore."

"Be careful out there," Clint said. "It can be kind of dangerous."

Franks hesitated, then turned and headed for the door.

"I think you scared him," the bartender said.

"Yeah," Clint said, "I hope so."

THIRTY

Clint crossed the street to return to the hotel. Loretta was still at the window. The stranger was riding hell-bent for leather out of town. He had to go and report that Clint was, indeed, in town, but what would he say about the chest? He couldn't tell if Clint had it or not.

By the time he got to Loretta's door, it was open and she was standing there, waiting.

"What happened?" she asked. "That man came running out and rode out of town like he was on fire."

"I introduced myself."

"You threatened him?"

"No," Clint said. "I introduced myself. That's all."

"And he ran like that?"

Clint nodded. "I'm going to my room," he said. "We need to get an early start in the morning."

"Why don't you come in and . . . and talk?" she asked.

"Loretta," he said, "get some rest. You must be sore from riding."

"I ride fairly often, actually," she said. "I'm fine."

"Okay," he said. "I'll go and get some rest. See you in the morning."

Clint walked to his room, entered without looking back, and closed his door.

Franks found Duffy's camp and dismounted before the horse stopped.

"What the hell—" Duffy said.

"No whores . . ." Franks said breathlessly. ". . . saw the Gunsmith . . . don't know about chest . . ."

"Hey, hey," Duffy said, "take it easy. What the hell happened?"

"Went to saloon . . ."

"Are you drunk?"

"No!"

"Here," Duffy said, pouring a cup of coffee, "drink this and sit down."

Franks sat down and caught his breath and then, while drinking the coffee, told Duffy about meeting the Gunsmith.

"He introduced himself to you?"

"Yeah."

"What were you doin'?"

"I was havin' a beer . . ."

"And?"

"And talkin'."

"About what?"

"About whores! What's the difference?"

"What did he say?"

"He said he saw me ride into town."

"And you went right to the saloon?"

"Yeah."

"And he came in right behind you."

"Yeah. We got any whiskey left?"

"No whiskey," Duffy said. "You've got first watch."

"Watch? What for?"

"Because if we both go to sleep," Duffy said, "the Gun-smith may slip up here and kill us in our sleep."

Franks looked at Duffy and said, "Naw."

"Oh, yeah. He knows you went in to scout around."

"How does he know that?"

"Because he's smart," Duffy said, "and you're not. You should've gone in and kept your mouth shut."

"I was looking for a whorehouse," Franks said. "They don't got one!"

"You got first watch," Duffy said. "Wake me if you hear anythin'. Understand?"

"I understand."

"If you fall asleep, we could both die. Got it?"

"I got it, Duffy!"

Idiot, Duffy thought.

Clint was lying on his bed, reading.

He spent a lot of time in hotel rooms this way, with his gun hanging on the bedpost. He even tried to read by campfire light when he was on the trail. His reading tended to be Twain, Dickens, and some other popular material.

There was a knock on the door, so light he missed it at first. When it came again, he got off the bed, grabbed his gun from the holster, and went to the door. When he opened it, he was surprised to see Loretta standing there.

"You okay?" he asked.

"I . . . wanted to talk," she said, shrugging.

"Well, okay," Clint said. "Come in."

She entered and he closed the door.

"Oh," she said, when she saw his gun. "I guess you answer the door like that . . . all the time?"

"Yes," he said, "all the time."

He walked to he bedpost and slid his gun back into its holster.

"What do you want to talk about?" he asked.

THIRTY-ONE

"I don't know," she said, sitting on the bed. "I just didn't want to be alone." She picked up the book he was reading. "Dickens?"

"Does that surprise you?"

"Actually, yes."

He took the book from her and set it on the table next to the bed. Then he sat, leaving a wide space between them. She was beautiful, she smelled good, and she was vulnerable. Better to keep some space between them.

"Clint . . ."

"Yes."

"Why are you sitting so far away?"

He didn't want to tell her what he was just thinking, so he tried to think of something else.

"I'm trying to be a gentleman."

"Well," she said, "you're being too much of a gentleman. The lady needs some . . . comfort."

"Comfort?"

"As in a hug?"

"Oh."

He scooted over on the bed and gave her a hug.

Duffy couldn't sleep.

If Clint Adams and the woman had found the chest, then they had it with them in that town. And they would need to find a way to get it back to Westbrook. So all he and Franks had to do was watch and wait for them to come riding out of Bolden with a buckboard.

Only if Adams knew he was being watched, he'd be on the alert. Thanks to Franks, Duffy was going to have to come up with a good plan.

Or a lot more men.

Clint hugged Loretta.

He was very aware of the heat of her body as she leaned into him.

"Thank you," she said.

"You're welcome."

"This is very helpful."

"Good."

They sat that way for a while, then she sort of lifted her face so that it was in the crook of his neck. He felt her breath hot on his skin, and felt his body reacting to her nearness.

Then he thought he felt her lips touch his neck.

"Loretta?"

"I thought you might need some comfort, too," she said, kissing his neck again.

"Damn it, Loretta!" he said.

He moved his head down and their lips met. Gently at first, and then more heated. Soon it was a molten kiss. Her hands were all over him. She got to her knees and pressed him down onto the bed aggressively.

"Lore—"

"Shut up, Clint," she said. "Just shut up!"

She pulled his shirt out of his pants, pulled it up, and began to kiss his chest and belly. Her hands worked feverishly on his belt, and then the buttons of his pants. She reached in and brought out his hard cock, and took it into her mouth. He was shocked.

Given her previous attitude about everything, he was surprised to find her sucking his hard cock with all the talent of an experienced whore.

"Jesus—" he said, then bit off the rest. Using her hands and her mouth, she had him close to bursting, and he had to use all his willpower not to explode into her mouth.

Not yet, anyway.

Duffy rolled out of his bedroll and walked over to the fire. Franks was sitting in front of it, but he was dozing.

Duffy took out his gun, put it near Franks's ear and cocked the hammer back.

Franks jumped, looked up at Duffy, and said, "I was awake."

"Yeah, I know. Go get some sleep."

"Is it time?"

"No, but I can't sleep, so go ahead."

"What's on your mind?"

"Gettin' some more men, that's what's on my mind," Duffy said.

"Who?"

"I don't know," Duffy said. "I'll give it some thought while I'm makin' coffee."

Franks nodded, and went to his bedroll. In minutes he was asleep and snoring.

Duffy made himself another pot of coffee, and started making a list in his head.

THIRTY-TWO

Loretta stripped Clint completely naked, then took the time to take off her own clothes.

"Too aggressive?" she asked him, running her hands up and down his thighs.

"No," he said, "just surprisingly so."

"I can be as wild as anyone when I want to," she said. "And tonight, I want to."

He reached for her and pulled her down on top of him. The nipples of her full breasts were hard against his chest.

They kissed avidly, and then she worked her way down his body until she had him in her mouth again. But this time he wasn't just going to lie there and take it. He pulled her up onto him, then flipped her over onto her back.

It was his turn to wander about her body with his hands and mouth, coming to rest with his face nestled in the damp heat between her legs.

"Oooh, yes," she said, reaching down to hold his head in place. "Like that. Right there. Oh, God."

He slid his hands beneath her to cup her ass and lift her off the bed. He worked on her with his lips and tongue until she was banging her fists on the mattress, then he mounted her and drove his penis into her. She almost screamed, and wrapped her legs around his waist as he pounded away at her . . .

Later, they lay side by side, naked, sweat drying on their bodies.

"That was . . . amazing."

"Surprising," he said.

"Yes," she said. She moved over and snuggled up against him.

"You mind if I sleep here tonight?" she asked. "I don't think I have the energy to go back to my room."

"I don't have the energy to say no," he replied.

"Mmmm," she said, reaching down between his legs to stroke him back to life.

"I thought you said you wanted to sleep?" he asked.

She laughed deep in her throat and threw one leg over him.

"We can sleep . . . later," she said.

Clint woke later with the weight of Loretta on his left arm. He reached to make sure he could still pull his gun if he had to, then settled in to sleep for the night. He doubted anyone would be coming to town after them, not until they had found the chest.

Sheriff Lane struck him as the ultimate opportunist, ready to take advantage of any situation at a moment's notice. He probably knew that Loretta had a thousand dollars on her, but he was going to be more interested in what was in that chest. They all knew that Loretta Burns wanted that chest for more than just a few dresses, or possessions that were inside.

He looked down at her, her naked, full breasts, her dark

brown nipples, her long supple legs. Was this her way of keeping his mind occupied? If it was, it also served to keep busy, as well.

Clint didn't trust Loretta any more than he trusted Sheriff Lane. Everybody had his own agenda, but he still couldn't leave her to face Lane and his men herself.

His agenda was to keep her alive long enough to have her show him what was in the chest.

THIRTY-THREE

Duffy kicked Franks awake in the morning.

"What the—"

"Get up!" he said. "You've got work to do."

"Yeah, okay," Franks said, getting to his feet. "What about some coffee?"

"Yeah, have yourself a cup of coffee," Duffy said. "Then we're gonna break camp and keep an eye out for Adams and the woman. Wanna see if they leave town emptyhanded, or with that chest."

"And if they have the chest?"

"It'll take them a while to get back to Westbrook with it," Duffy said. "Before they do, we'll take it away from them."

"And the five hundred dollars?"

"Right," Duffy said, "and the five hundred dollars."

"Duffy, you think maybe I can get more than a hundred of that?"

"No," Duffy said. "Get your coffee, and then get your horse saddled."

* * *

As Clint and Loretta rode out of Bolden, he knew they were being watched from somewhere. It was only a matter of time before he spotted the men.

"Couldn't we have slept a little longer?" she asked. "You tired me out last night."

"I think it was the other way around. If I remember right, you interrupted my reading."

"I didn't hear you complaining."

"Well, you're complaining now," he said. "It's pretty clear to me that Sheriff Lane has sent someone after us."

"For my money?"

"And for your box."

"What does he care about the chest?" she asked.

"He's curious, Loretta," Clint said. "About what's inside. He assumes it's something of value."

"Well, yes," she said, "but to me, not to anyone else."

He didn't know if she was telling the truth.

"Well, he's going to want to see that for himself," he said.

"And you figured this out how? Because a stranger came to town last night?"

"And left quickly when he found out who I was."

"Haven't people done that before?"

"Yes," he said, "but in this case, I don't think he went very far. He and at least one partner are probably watching us right now. Don't look around!"

She stopped herself just in time.

"What will they do when they see us leaving without the chest?"

"Follow us," Clint said.

"Until we find it."

"Yes."

"And then they'll take it away from us?"

"They'll try," Clint answered.

"Can we lose them?"

"It's possible," he said, "depending on how many there are."

"So we have to lose them, and then find my chest."

"The black box."

"My black box."

"Do we really need it?"

"Need what?"

"The whole thing?" he asked. "The whole black chest?"

"Why not?"

"Well, I just thought, maybe, there was just something inside you wanted."

"It's all my stuff," she said. "Everything inside belongs to me. I'm not letting anyone else have any part of it."

"Well," he said, "it was just a thought."

From a hill outside of town, Duffy and Frank watched them ride out of Bolden.

"They don't have it," Franks said.

"Not yet."

"So what do we do?"

"There's no hurry," Duffy said. "We'll follow them. And first chance we get, I'll send a telegram."

"For more men?"

"Yes."

"That's not gonna cost me any of my money, is it?" Franks asked.

Only all of it, Duffy thought.

"No."

They rode for half a day, bypassed two other towns, and stopped to rest.

"Are they behind us?" she asked as she took a drink from her canteen.

"Yes."

"You can see them?"

"I can feel them."

She lowered her canteen and looked at him.

"Really?"

"Yes."

"How can that be?"

"It comes from years of experience."

She hung her canteen back on her saddle. "So how do we lose them?"

"I'll figure out a way," he said. "Soon."

"Meanwhile," she said, "how far to the stage station?"

"Half a day, maybe less, if we ride straight for it and stop trying to find the chest."

"What?"

"If we assume the chest was still on the stage when you stopped at the station, we can simply head there."

"And what if the box fell off between here and there?"

"Well, if it's out in the open, we'll see it."

"And?"

"And if we get to the station and the stationmaster says the chest was there when the stage was, we double back."

"This doesn't sound like a well-thought-out plan to me."

"On the other hand," he said, "whoever's following us is probably expecting us to stop at the station. Why don't they just go there?"

"Maybe," she said, "they already have men there."

Clint hung his own canteen on his saddle. "Let's hope they don't think of that."

Franks turned when he heard a rider approaching. He saw Duffy riding up on him.

"Did you do it?"

"Yeah," Duffy said. "That town had a telegraph key."

"So what did you do?"

"I sent some men on ahead," Duffy said. "They'll be waitin' for us—and them—when we get there."

"How many?"

"Just two," Duffy said, "but it should be enough."

"So we keep following?"

Duffy nodded. "At a safe distance."

THIRTY-FOUR

The station was up ahead.

"That's it," she said. "I recognize it."

"Not much to recognize," he said. "They all pretty much look alike."

It was just a wooden building with a corral behind it, a small stable, and a buckboard. There must have been a horse or two inside the stable.

"Who was here?" Clint asked.

"Just one man and a woman, his wife. She cooked for us."

"That's her job."

They sat their horses a bit longer, looking around.

"It's quiet," he said. "Too quiet."

"Well, when there's no stage maybe they just . . . stay inside."

"Should be some horses in the corral," he said. "Replacements, in case a stage arrives with a damaged horse."

"So why aren't there?"

"That's what I'm going to find out," Clint said. "You stay here."

He dismounted and handed her Eclipse's reins, even though it wasn't necessary.

"I'll be right back."

Once Duffy realized they were going to the station, next he dropped back even more.

"What are we doin'?" Franks asked.

"Just playin' it safe," Duffy said. "Adams is nobody's fool."

"But what about the men you sent?" Franks asked. "Won't they be there?"

"I hope so," Duffy said. "And I hope they stay out of sight. I told them not to go in."

"Will they listen?"

"Do you?"

"Well . . ."

Inside the building Angus Foster and his wife, Mary, sat at the long wooden table and looked at the two who had broken in only an hour before.

"Look," Angus said, "we don't have any money—"

"Shut up!" one of them said.

"I could make some food," Mary said.

"Be quiet!" the other one said.

"We weren't supposed to come in here," Rory Evans said to his partner, Andy King.

"Never mind," King said. "We're better off in here, where Adams can't see us."

"That ain't what Duffy said," Evans replied, lowering his voice.

"Go take a look out the window," King said. "See if anyone's comin'."

"Yeah, okay."

Evans walked to the window. King turned to the older

couple and said, "Just be quiet, and everythin' will be fine. Understand?"

"We understand," Angus Foster said. "Don't we, Mother?"

Mary looked at her husband and said, "Actually, not at all, Angus."

Clint moved in toward the house and stable, with intentions of first looking in the stable. When he reached it, he moved slowly. If there were horses inside, he did not want to spook them.

As he moved around the stable, he saw there was only a front door. There was, however, space between the slats that made up the structure. He tried to peer into the interior that way, to make out what was inside, but couldn't see much. He was going to have to move around to the front and look in the door. If he did that, there was the possibility he could be seen from the house, but he decided to take the chance.

He figured if there was anyone in the house, they'd be keeping an eye out the front window. He moved around the side of the stable. There was one window in the back, and there didn't seem to be anyone standing at it. He made his move toward the door and peered in, then stepped inside.

The interior was dark, the only light coming from that front door. After a few moments, he was able to see well enough to spot three horses, a couple of them still wearing their saddles. He moved alongside the two saddle mounts, found them still wet. They'd been ridden in the past hour or so. Likely the two riders were inside the house.

There were some hay bales in one corner of the the stable, probably used to feed the stock.

He went through their saddlebags but didn't find anything informative. Their rifles were gone, though. He could only surmise that there were two men inside the house, waiting for them. Now the question was, were they the two men who had been following them, who had perhaps circled around to get there first. Or were these two additional men? Worst-case scenario, there were now four men to be dealt with.

He moved to the door, peered out to make sure no one was looking out the window of the house. He had two choices. Go back and rejoin Loretta, or get close to the house and take a look in that rear window.

Since he had made his way this far, he decided to get a look inside the house.

From her vantage point, still holding Clint's horse, Loretta was able to see when Clint slipped into the stable, and again when he reappeared at the door. But when he came out he didn't head back to her. Instead, he went toward the house. She was nervous, not knowing who was going to come up behind her. She kept looking back nervously, while trying to also keep an eye on what Clint was doing.

She didn't have a gun, but her eyes fell on Clint's rifle, which he had left behind.

THIRTY-FIVE

When Duffy and Franks came within sight of the station, they also saw the girl, sitting on her horse alone, holding the reins of Clint Adams's horse.

"We could grab her," Franks said.

"I'm thinkin' of that," Duffy said. "Looks like those two idiots went into the house, which I told them not to do."

"Where's Adams?" Franks asked, standing in his stirrups. "I don't see him."

"He's gotta be down there," Duffy said. "Maybe we should take the girl now."

"I can go down and get 'er," Franks said.

"Just hold on," Duffy said. "Don't rush into anythin'. Just sit tight a minute, lemme think."

Impatiently, Franks settled into his saddle.

Clint covered the ground between the stable and the house, pressed himself against the back wall. He listened for a moment but didn't hear any voices, so he risked a look in the back window. The house was just one room, so he was able to see everything inside. There was an older couple sitting at the table, probably the station manager and his wife. And with them were two armed men, one of whom was looking out the front window.

Waiting for him, no doubt.

Duffy couldn't see the back wall, but he had seen Clint leave the stable.

"He's gonna take 'em," he said. "Let's go."

"We takin' the girl?"

"Yeah," Duffy said.

"What about the chest?"

"We'll keep lookin' for it," Duffy said. "This is a chance to get the drop on Clint Adams."

"Okay," the eager Franks said.

"Just take it easy," Duffy said. "I don't wanna spook her. Understand?"

"Sure, I understand," Franks said. "Don't spook her. I ain't stupid."

Duffy certainly didn't agree with that.

Clint had two options.

He could break the glass on the back window and get the drop on the two men, but he'd be in an awkward position, and the two people at the table would be at risk.

If he went around to the front and got in the front door he could get the drop on them and wouldn't have the back wall between them.

He decided to work his way around to the front, try to get to the front door without being seen.

Inside, Andy King said to Rory Evans, "Check out that back window. We don't want anybody comin' up behind us."

"Right."

Angus Foster watched the two men carefully, waiting for

a chance to make a move. There was a gun in the room, and only he and his wife knew where it was. But Mary put her hand on Angus's wrist and shook her head. She did not want a dead hero for a husband.

Evans looked out the back window and said, "Nothin' out here."

"Keep watch," King said. "He may show up."

"What are the two of us gonna do against the Gunsmith, Andy?" Evans complained.

"Don't worry," King said. "We got hostages, and Duffy will be along soon. We'll let him deal with Adams."

"I don't know—"

"Just keep watch," King said, "and don't try to think, Rory."

Duffy and Franks moved up behind Loretta Burns, saw that she was holding a rifle.

"See how she holds it?" Duffy said in a low voice.

"She's got no idea how to use it. Just stay here and keep watch."

Duffy dismounted, handed Franks the reins of his horse, then started to move in closer on foot.

Clint moved around a side wall. From there, he was able to use a window to spot the two men inside. It looked like he could make it to the door without being seen. One of the men was now looking out the back window, although it was way too late.

He slid around to the front and started to inch toward the door.

THIRTY-SIX

Duffy snuck up behind Loretta, who was completely unaware, and grabbed the barrel of the rifle. She had her finger on the trigger, so as he yanked it from her hand, it went off.

Inside the house the two men heard the shot.

"What the hell—" Evans said from the back window.

"What was that?" King said loudly.

He peered intently out the front window, joined there by his partner.

Angus Foster decided to make his move, despite what his wife thought.

Clint froze. He was about to kick the door in when the shot rang out. He now had to worry about Loretta. She was either in danger, or she had fired a warning shot with his rifle.

He rushed the door, drew his gun, and kicked it in.

When the door slammed open, both King and Evans turned toward it.

Clint had no intention of firing, but an old-timer had

a gun in his hand and he started pulling the trigger. He winged one of the men, but the rest of his shots—six in all—missed. Clint had no choice but to fire, putting both men on the floor.

"We got 'em, goddamnit!" the old man shouted. "That was nice shootin', sonny."

"You crazy old man!" Mary Foster said, standing up and facing her husband.

"Keep quiet, woman!" Angus said. He looked at Clint. "You wanna tell us what's goin' on, mister? Them two busted in on us with their guns out, and wouldn't tell us nothin'."

"Not right now, old-timer," Clint said, reloading his gun. "There's something else going on outside."

"Ya mean that shot we heard?"

"Yes. You two better stay inside."

"Just lemme reload and I can go with—"

"You hush, old man!" Mary said. "You ain't goin' nowhere."

"Your wife is right," Clint said. "Just stay inside, folks."

Gun in hand, Clint stepped back outside.

Duffy cried out as Loretta pulled the trigger. He pulled the rifle from her grasp, and then dropped it as the barrel burned his hand.

"Damn it!" he said.

"What—"

He grabbed her and yanked her from the saddle.

"Let me go!" she shouted.

"Shut up!" he shouted back.

He held her with one hand and waved to Franks with the other. When he reached them he dismounted, and Duffy pushed the girl over to him.

"You hang onto her," Duffy said.

"My pleasure," Franks said. He put one arm around the woman's waist and pulled her tightly to his body. She could feel his excitement through his trousers.

"I'm gonna go down and talk to Adams."

"You gonna take 'im?" Franks asked.

"Not today," Duffy said. "We're still lookin' for that chest."

"Why do you want my chest?" Loretta demanded.

"I want this chest," Franks said, grabbing her breasts with his other hand.

"Cut that out!" Duffy said. "Just hold her. Don't do anythin' else."

"Yeah okay," Frank said, taking his hand away.

"Lady, you wanna tell us where that black chest of yours is?"

"I don't know!"

"Okay, then just tell us what's in it?"

"My dresses," she said, "and my underwear. Why is everybody so interested in my underwear."

"There's more than clothes in there or you wouldn't be out here lookin' for it with the Gunsmith," Duffy said.

"I don't know what you mean."

"You're full of crap," Duffy said. "Okay, Franks, just hold her here and don't do anythin', understand? I'm gonna talk to Adams."

"Yeah, okay."

"You don't have to hang on to her," Duffy said. "If she tries to get away, shoot her in the leg."

"Okay," Franks said, releasing her and smiling.

Loretta stumbled forward as he let her go, then turned and said to him, "You wouldn't dare!"

Franks grinned and said, "Try me."

THIRTY-SEVEN

Duffy made his way down to the station. Clint came out the front door and stood there with his gun in his hand. As Duffy approached, Clint holstered his gun, because Duffy's hands were empty.

"Adams?" Duffy asked.

"That's right."

"And my men?"

"Both dead."

Duffy shook his head. "Idiots. I told them to stay outside."

"What's your name?"

"Duffy," Duffy said. He never said his first name if he didn't have to.

"What's on your mind, Duffy? Is the woman okay?" Clint asked.

"She's okay," Duffy said. "She's with a friend of mine."

"So what do you want?"

"I think you know."

"Her money?"

"That," Duffy said, "and more."

"The chest."

"Now you got it."

"Sheriff Lane send you after us?"

"That don't matter," Duffy said.

"Well, look, if you want to trade the lady for the box, I don't have it."

"But you came here lookin' for it," Duffy said. "Why don't we go inside and ask your questions?"

"Sure, why not?" Clint asked.

He turned and went back inside, followed by Duffy.

"Who's this jasper?" Angus demanded.

"Never mind that," Clint said. "What are your names?"

"I'm Angus Foster, this is my Mrs."

"Mary," she said. "I have a name."

"Well, Mr. and Mrs. Foster, the last stage that came through here had a black chest on it. Or it did when it left."

"Came through here a few days ago," Angus said.

"Right. What we want to know is, did you notice a big black chest packed on the back of it?"

"Not on top?" Mary Foster asked.

"Naw," Angus said, "that stage was packed full. The rack on top was overflowing, so they tied some stuff on the back."

"And one of those was a black chest," Duffy said. "A big one."

"Why's everybody interested in this black box?" Angus asked.

"Because it wasn't on the stage when it arrived in Westbrook," Clint said.

The old man closed one eye and peered owlishly at Clint.

"You sayin' I stole it?"

"No," Clint said, "I'm asking you if either of you saw it."

"I didn't see anything," Mary said. "I stay inside and cook for the passengers and the driver."

"What about you?" Clint asked Angus. "You check the

rig and the horses, make sure everything's okay, exchange horses if you have to?"

"I did all that," the old man said. "I didn't see no chest."

"Okay," Duffy said, "you're sayin' it wasn't there?"

"I'm sayin' I didn't notice if it was or wasn't," Angus said.

"You don't check the bags?" Clint asked. "Make sure they're cinched in tight?"

"Ain't my job," Angus said. "They want me to do that, they're gonna have to pay me more."

Duffy looked around the room, glanced at the two men on the floor.

"They work for you?" Angus asked.

"Yes."

"Not no more," he said, and cackled.

"You silly old man," Mary said, "you missed them with every shot."

"I did not!" Angus said. He looked at Clint. "Did I?"

"You winged one of them," Clint admitted.

"See?' Angus said to his wife. "I winged one of them."

"By accident," Mary said.

Clint and Duffy left the older couple to their argument and stepped outside.

"Maybe we should look around," Duffy suggested. "The old man may have stolen it, after all."

"How would he have gotten it off the stage?" Clint asked.

"Maybe the driver helped him."

"Why would they take that one chest?" Clint asked.

"I dunno," Duffy said. "Maybe they steal one bag from every stage, hoping it's got somethin' valuable in it."

"Well," Clint said, "I was in the stable, and it's not there. And it's not in the house. So where else would it be?"

THIRTY-EIGHT

"I want the woman," Clint said.

"Yeah, you do."

"I don't have the chest to give you in exchange."

"No, you ain't."

"So what do we do?" Clint asked.

"You find the chest," Duffy said. "When you do, we'll trade."

"What are you going do with her in the meantime?" Clint asked.

"Treat her well," Duffy said. "With respect."

"Where?"

"I don't know," Duffy said. "We'll figure that out."

"Why don't we all just stay together?" Clint suggested.

"Partners?" Duffy asked.

"Not really," Clint said, "but if you want to think of it that way . . ."

"You think you'll be able to take me along the way?" Duffy asked. "If we're gonna do that, I'll need your gun."

Not a chance," Clint said. "The minute I give up my gun, I'm dead."

"You don't trust me?"

"Don't feel bad," Clint said. "I don't trust anyone enough to give up my gun."

"I guess I don't blame you, with your reputation," Duffy said. "Okay, so why don't you keep lookin' and we'll keep the girl."

"I can't go along with that," Clint said. "Give me the girl."

"And then what do we do?"

"Keep following us," Clint said. "When we find the chest, you'll know."

"And then what?"

"Then you can make your move."

"I don't like that," Duffy said.

"You want what's in the chest," Clint said.

"We want what's valuable in the chest."

"*If* there's anything valuable in there," Clint said.

"There's got to be," Duffy said, "or you two wouldn't be out here."

"Then why don't you go out and look for it?" Clint asked. "Try to get to it before we do."

"Like a contest?"

"Right."

"No."

"Then I've got another idea," Clint said.

"What's that?"

"Go for your gun," Clint said, "now."

"I can pay you to let me go," Loretta said to Franks.

"Shut up."

They were both watching Clint and Duffy, who were standing out in front of the station.

"What are you getting paid for this?" she asked. "I can double it. Triple it."

"I said—"

He turned his head to look at her. She had taken the roll of money out of her bag and was holding it.

"This is a thousand dollars," she said. "It's yours. And I can get you more when we get back to town."

"A thousand?"

"That's right."

Duffy had told him the woman had five hundred dollars on her, and was going to give him a hundred of it.

And she had a thousand?

"I like the idea," Duffy said, "but not right now."

"Why, because you're working for the sheriff?" Clint asked. "What's he paying you? You can't tell me you're not thinking about keeping for yourself whatever's in the chest."

"And you don't know what's in it?" Duffy asked.

"She hasn't told me," Clint said. "Ever since what happened in town, I don't think she trusts anybody."

"Not even the great Gunsmith?"

Clint laughed. "She didn't even know who I was," he said. "I had to tell her."

"That bother you?"

"No," Clint said. "It interested me."

Duffy turned and looked behind him. Clint assumed he was looking up to where he'd left Loretta with his partner.

"We're not getting anywhere," Clint said. "I'm not going to let you leave here with her. That's not an option. I'd rather kill you."

"And then my friend will kill her."

"And then I'll kill him. And then what happens?" Clint smiled. "I get the money and the chest."

THIRTY-NINE

Duffy walked up to where Franks was with the girl.

"What're we doin?" Franks asked.

"Let 'er go."

"What?"

Duffy looked at Loretta.

"You can go down there," Duffy told her. "Take both horses with you."

"Really?"

"Yes," Duffy said. "Go!"

"What's goin' on?" Franks demanded.

Duffy held his hand up to him to shut him up. Loretta grabbed the reins of both horses and started walking them toward the station.

"What's goin' on?" Franks asked.

"Adams and I came to an understanding."

"And what's that?"

"Him and the girl will keep lookin' for the box, and we'll keep watchin' them."

"What?"

"It was the only way we don't all end up dead," Duffy said. "Especially you."

"Me? Why me?"

"I don't know," Duffy said. "But he said he wanted to kill you."

"Wha—"

Duffy smacked him on the shoulder and said, "I saved your life."

Loretta approached Clint, then dropped the reins and pressed her forehead to his chest.

"You okay?" he asked.

"I'm fine."

"They didn't . . . touch you?"

"No." She stepped back and looked at him. "How did you do that? Get them to let me go?"

"I just explained the situation," he said.

"So they're going to leave us alone?"

"No," Clint said. "We're going back to the way things were."

"Status quo."

"Right."

"Why?"

"Because nobody dies that way." He picked up the horse's reins. "Why don't you go inside? Maybe we can get Mary to make us something to eat."

"Mary?"

"Go on inside and introduce yourself," Clint said. "I'll be right there."

She went inside. He walked the two horses to the stable. With three horses inside, it was already too crowded, so he just tied them outside. He'd have to decide what to do with the two dead men's horses.

Oh yeah, and the dead men.

* * *

Loretta had to step over the two bodies to get into the house.

"I'm Loretta," she said.

"I'm Mary, honey," the old woman said. "You and your man was somethin' to eat?"

"He's not my man," Loretta said, "but we could still use something to eat."

"Comin' up." Mary turned to Angus. "Old man, you and that other fella get these bodies out of here!"

"Yes, ma'am."

FORTY

While Clint and Angus buried the bodies, Mary—with Loretta's help—whipped up a meal of tortillas and beans.

"It's easy to make," Mary said when Clint asked why she was making Mexican food.

While they ate, Clint again asked Angus to try and remember if the chest was on the stage when it pulled in.

"If it was on when they pulled in," Angus said, "it was on when they pulled out. And if it wasn't there when they pulled in . . ."

"I get it," Clint said.

The tortillas were good, so he paid attention to them.

"They're probably eatin' good in there," Franks said. "We should go down."

"That wasn't part of the deal," Duffy said. "Drink your coffee and eat your jerky."

They were sitting across the fire from each other.

"She has a thousand dollars on her," Franks said. "Did you know that?"

"I thought it was five hundred."

"I saw it," Franks said.

"Did you count it?"

"I didn't have to," he said. "It was a big roll."

"She offered it to you, and you didn't take it?" Duffy asked. "Why?"

"Because I knew you'd kill me, that's why," Franks said. "Besides, I still want my cut of what's in that chest."

"Your cut?" Duffy asked.

"Yeah," Franks said, "I think maybe I deserve a cut now."

Duffy thought that over and said, "Yeah, maybe you do."

"And I think maybe we should just cut Sheriff Lane out."

"Lane won't like that."

"Yeah, but you can handle him," Franks said. "Look how you made a deal with Adams."

Duffy thought Franks might have been getting a little too secure.

"I can take care of everybody," Duffy said. "Don't forget that."

"You figurin' on spendin' the night?" Angus asked. "We ain't outfitted for overnight guests."

"No," Clint said. "We still have some daylight. We'll move on."

"Good."

While Mary washed dishes, Angus went outside, leaving Clint and Loretta sitting at the table.

"Are you sure you don't need help, Mary?" Loretta asked.

"You just sit tight, honey," Mary said. "You been through an ordeal."

"So has she," Clint said to Loretta.

"Doesn't seem to have bothered her any," Loretta said. "She's pretty tough."

"Yep, she is."

Clint poured himself some more of Mary's good coffee. He offered Loretta some, but she shook her head.

"Where do we go now?" she asked.

"We keep looking," Clint said, "keep backtracking the stage."

"What about the last few miles we sort of . . . over-looked?"

"I think Duffy and his man might have seen it if we missed it," Clint said. "They didn't."

"What about Angus and Mary?" she asked.

"You think this little old couple stole your chest off the back of the stage?" he asked. "How did they get it off?"

"Just untie it and . . . let it drop."

"And nobody noticed?"

"Hey," she said, "it did drop off somewhere and nobody noticed."

"While in motion," Clint said. "If it was just sitting out there, I think somebody would've noticed."

"So we're back to where we started," she said.

"Not really," he replied. "We've eliminated all the miles between here and Westbrook. By the way, where did you catch the stage?"

"St. Joe."

"Missouri?"

She nodded.

"That's a lot of ground to cover."

"Yes, it is."

"So the sooner we get started," Clint said, "the better."

FORTY-ONE

Clint and Loretta said goodbye to Angus and Mary and went to the stable to get their horses. Loretta looked up to where she knew Duffy and his man were.

"What about them?" she asked.

"What *about* them?"

"What if they just decide to shoot us from there, with rifles?"

"They'd have to be really good."

"Maybe they are."

"They don't want to kill us," Clint said, checking Eclipse's legs. "They want to find that chest."

"Jesus," she said, "it's *my* chest. Doesn't anybody understand that?"

"Everybody understands that, Loretta," he said, checking her horse's legs, "it's just that nobody cares."

"Can we outrun them?" she asked.

"I can," Clint said, looking at her. "You can't."

"What if I take one of their horses," she said, pointing into the stable.

Clint looked in at the two horses. Either one would have been better than what she was riding now.

"That's an idea."

"Should we change saddles?"

"No," he said, "even their saddles are better than yours."

They walked into the stable.

"Which one should I take?" she asked.

"This steel dust is only about five, and will run fast," he said. "Up you go."

"What are they doin'?" Franks asked.

"Getting ready to leave, obviously," Duffy said.

"Yeah, but it looks like they're switchin' horses."

Duffy finished kicking the fire to death and took a look.

"Looks like they're takin' King's steel dust," he said.

"It's better than what she was ridin'," Franks observed.

"Yeah," Duffy said. "And faster."

"So?"

"With that horse, and Adams's, they can outrun us."

"You think they'd try that?" Franks asked.

"They might."

"Then why don't we put a bullet into that big black horse of his right now?"

"That's a sound idea, except for one thing," Duffy said.

"What?"

"You kill his horse, he'll never rest until we're dead."

"Then shoot the steel dust."

"Can you hit it from here?" Duffy asked.

"I don't know," Franks said. "Can't you?"

"Maybe," Duffy said. "I'm better with a pistol."

"So what do we do?"

Duffy frowned. "I'll think of somethin'."

They walked the steel dust out, put Loretta's mare inside.

"Are we gonna leave them there?" she asked.

"The stage line can probably use them."

They mounted up and headed away from the station.

"They can see what we're doing," she said.

"Hopefully they'll just think we're swapping for a better horse."

"When do we run?"

"I'll tell you," Clint said. "For now, just relax. Get used to the new horse."

"It feels good," she said, bouncing in the saddle. "Stronger."

"Don't bounce," Clint said, "just ride."

They followed the road, which was filled with old ruts from the passing of previous stages over the days, or weeks. But Clint could tell which of the ruts were fresher.

"Are we going to follow the trail all the way back to St. Jo?" she asked.

"Isn't that what you want to do?"

"No," she said, "I want to find it long before that."

"Maybe the next station," Clint said, "wherever that is."

They rode a few more miles and then Clint called their progress to a halt.

"What is it?"

"Marks," he said, pointing. "The chest fell off here, was dragged that way."

He dismounted, walked to the side of the road. The drag marks continued through the brush.

"What is it?"

"Somebody hooked the chest up to the back of a horse or a mule and dragged it."

"To where?"

"That's what we're going to find out," he said. "Dismount. We're going to walk."

FORTY-TWO

The drag marks went through brush, a gulley, a field, anywhere there was no road. Whoever had taken the thing had wanted to hide the tracks as much as possible.

"Who do you think took it?" Loretta asked.

"Somebody who didn't have the strength to lift it up onto a buckboard."

"So they had to drag it like this."

"Yes."

"Back toward the station."

"Looks like."

"That means . . ."

"Angus and Mary."

"I don't think that nice old lady knew anything about it," Loretta said.

"That nice old lady knows every move her man makes," Clint said. "Believe me."

"Where did they put it, then?"

"That's what we're going to find out."

* * *

"What are they doin'?" Franks said.

"Ain't it obvious?" Duffy asked. "They're following a trail."

"Off the road?"

"Someone dragged the box off the road," Duffy said.

"To where?"

Well, it looks like . . . back toward the station."

"Maybe we should go there?" Franks said.

"No," Duffy replied, "we'll keep followin' them."

"But . . . they know we're followin' them. Maybe they're just . . . tryin' to fool us?"

"Well see, Dennis," Duffy said. "We'll see.

"I can't believe that old couple stole my chest," Loretta said.

"I think it was like you said, Loretta," Clint said. "The box fell off. Somehow, old Angus found it and—probably with Mary's help—dragged it somewhere. Tell me something."

"What?"

"How hard will it be to open without a key?"

"It's like a safe."

"Then, maybe they haven't gotten it open yet."

They followed the drag marks a bit farther and then Clint said, "Yeah, they're leading us right back to the station. Let's go."

They mounted up and quickened their pace.

"Damnit, Angus," Mary said. "it's been days and you ain't got it opened yet. I don't even know why you brought it here."

Angus looked up at his wife, who was looming over him as he tried to open the chest with a hammer.

"Can't you stop railin' at me, woman?"

"Why don't you just get an axe."

"This chest is made of extremely hard wood," Angus said, "and our axe is dull as a spoon."

"Those people could come back any time, Angus," Mary said. "Maybe we should've given the lady her box back."

"Look," Angus said, "Eddie told me the box fell off, instead of going back to get it. We're supposed to split what's in it with him when he comes back this way."

"That thief!" she said. "We never should've got involved with his schemes. What if there's nothing in there but . . . unmentionables?"

"Then we'll get rid of it," Angus said. He stood up. "I'm gonna get my shotgun!"

As Angus and Mary left the stable, they stopped short. Clint and Loretta were staring down at them from their horses.

"You won't need a shotgun, or an axe," Loretta said. "I have the key."

FORTY-THREE

"Maybe," Loretta said, "we should call down those two men so they can also get a look inside the chest."

"Do you want to do that?"

"Why not?" she asked. "Let's just show everybody what's in the chest."

Clint turned in his saddle and waved his arms.

"Duffy," he called out, "bring your man down!"

"What the—" Dennis Franks said. "Why's he callin' us?"

"I think," Duffy said, "we're finally gonna get a look inside the black box."

He started his horse down the hill, followed by Franks.

"What's goin' on, Adams?" Duffy asked.

"We're all about to get a look inside this box that's caused us much trouble, thanks to the generosity of Miss Burns."

Loretta held the key up so they could all see it.

The two men dismounted.

"We can't all go inside the stable," Clint said. "Duffy, you and your man can help her drag the box out here."

"Why are there no drag marks out here?" Loretta asked.

"I'm willing to bet they dragged it around back, got it into the stable, and then rubbed out the marks."

Angus looked away. Mary bit her lip.

"Let's get it out here," Duffy said. "I want to see what's in it."

Clint and the two men went inside and, with little difficulty since there was three of them, dragged the box outside.

"This looks specially made," Clint said.

"It is," Loretta said. "I told you, it's like a safe. It was built to resist any attempts to open it."

"And to survive accidents," Clint said, "like falling off the back of the stage."

"Are we gonna open it?" Franks asked, hand on his gun.

"Duffy, tell your man to take his hand away from his gun," Clint said warningly.

"Franks!" Duffy snapped.

Franks dropped his hand to his side.

"Loretta," Clint said. "This box is yours. If you don't want to open it, that's your right. We'll just arrange to have it taken to Westbrook."

"Adams—" Duffy said.

"No, it's okay," Loretta said. "Maybe if I'd just told everyone why I wanted the box in the first place, none of this would have happened."

"So there *is* somethin' valuable in the box?" Duffy asked.

"Somethin' other than . . . unmentionables?" Angus asked.

"There's something valuable in here," Loretta said, crouching down by the box, "but only to me, and one other person."

"Who?" Clint asked.

Loretta didn't answer. She slid the solid brass key into the lock of the box and turned it. The group heard the lock disengage.

Loretta tucked the key away, reached out for the heavy lid, and lifted it open. Everyone around her leaned in to look.

FORTY-FOUR

Loretta reached into the chest and came out with a framed photograph of a man.

"This is it," she said.

"What?" Duffy said.

"W-what the hell—" Franks sputtered.

Mary swatted her husband and said, "I tol' you so!"

"Who is it?" Clint asked.

"My father," she said. "It's the only photograph ever taken of him."

"You said it was valuable to one other person?"

"Yes," she said, hugging it to her chest, "my brother, Randolph. I think he'll be coming after me for it."

"Are you afraid of him?" Clint asked.

"He would kill me for this," she said.

Duffy backed away from the assemblage, and Franks followed.

"This ain't right," Duffy said. "You wouldn't be runnin' around out here lookin' for that if all you wanted was a picture."

Loretta looked up at Duffy.

"I'm sorry, but this is it. Do you want to go through the rest of the box yourself? There's nothing in it but my personal belongings."

"Go through it, Dennis," Duffy said.

Loretta got to her feet and moved away. Clint made a move to intercept Franks, but Loretta said, "No, Clint, let him."

Clint stepped back.

Franks delved into the chest, began moving frilly things around, digging down to the bottom of the chest. Clint gave him credit for not dumping things on the ground.

"Nothin'," Franks said, looking up at Duffy. "There ain't nothin' here. No money, no gold, nothin'!"

He stood up, backed away to stand next to Duffy.

"Satisfied?" Clint asked Duffy.

Duffy stared at Clint.

"The money."

"What?" Clint asked.

"The thousand dollars she's carryin'," Duffy said. "I want it."

Clint laughed. "If that's all you go back to Sheriff Lane with, he's not going to like it."

Duffy fumed.

"On the other hand, if we all go back and explain the situation to him, maybe he'll believe us."

Franks looked at Duffy to see if he was buying this. Because he wasn't.

"Duffy, a thousand dollars is a lot of money," he said. "We can split it. Lane don't have to know."

Clint studied Duffy's face.

"Maybe Duffy doesn't want to split it with you, friend," Clint said. "Ever think of that?"

Franks bit his lip.

"You told me she had five hundred, and you was gonna

pay me a hundred. A hundred! When all the time you knew she had a thousand!"

"Shut up, Franks," Duffy said. "He's just tryin' to divide us. We can take him together."

Angus and Mary suddenly moved away, taking Loretta with them.

"Wha—" Loretta said as they wedged her between them.

"This is gonna get ugly, missy," Mary said.

"Make it easy, Adams," Duffy said. "Give us the thousand."

"Let them have it, Clint!" Loretta said.

"Sorry, I can't do that," Clint said. "They won't be satisfied with it. They think they'll kill me, take the thousand, and then take you back to get them more. Or maybe they'll kill you after they kill me."

"Shut up," Duffy said. He stepped a few feet away from Franks, who stayed where he was. "Give us the money, missy, or we'll kill Adams."

"Just relax, Loretta."

"I'll give you the money!" Loretta shouted.

"I won't," Clint said.

"You're makin' this hard," Duffy said.

"Yeah," Clint said. "On you."

"H-he ain't backin' off, Duffy," Franks said. "We got him two to one and he ain't backin' off."

"Shut up!" Duffy said.

Franks licked his lips and acquired a twitch in his left eye.

"Is a thousand dollars worth dying for?" Clint asked. The question was for either one of them.

"Damn you," Duffy said, and drew.

Clumsily, Franks also went for his gun.

Loretta's sharp intake of breath was very audible, followed by two quick shots.

"Gaw-damn!" Angus Foster said.

FORTY-FIVE

Clint and Loretta drove into Westbrook with the chest on a buckboard. Clint was driving, Eclipse was tied to the rear.

They drove much of the way in silence. Loretta had seen two men gunned down in front of her, and did not seem to be reacting well. Clint was thinking about how things had worked out, and he wasn't reacting well, either. He had ended up killing two men over a framed photograph.

On the bed of the buckboard, firmly tied down, was the black chest that everyone was so curious about.

Sheriff Lane came out of his office, saw Clint and Loretta riding in, and nodded his head. Duffy was nowhere to be found. That was what he'd expected. He'd had little or no confidence in Duffy being able to outdraw the Gunsmith. Of course, the man could always have gotten lucky. But in the end Lane had always felt he'd have to deal with the Gunsmith himself.

Clint pulled the buckboard to a stop in front of the hotel. He stepped down, and helped Loretta.

"I'll get some men to take the chest to your room," he said. "You can go and wait there."

"All right, Clint."

As she went inside, Clint thought this was an entirely different woman than the one who had gotten off the stage the other day.

Too different.

Clint found two men on the street who wanted to make a dollar each. They were about to take the chest off the buckboard when Sheriff Lane came over.

"Looks like you found it in one piece," he said.

"It's well made," Clint said. "It can take a lot of abuse."

"Like somebody tryin' to open it?"

"Exactly."

"You got it into town pretty easy, Adams," Lane said. "Gonna be a lot harder to get it out of town."

"I don't think so, Sheriff."

"Why's that?"

"I think you'll change your mind once you see what's inside."

Lane's eyes widened. "You already looked?"

Clint nodded. "So did your man Duffy, only he made a bad decision right after that. He won't be coming back."

Lane chuckled and said, "That don't surprise me."

The two men got the box off the buckboard with a grunt.

"Excuse me," Clint said. "I've got to make sure they get the chest to Miss Burns's room."

"That's fine with me," the sheriff said. "I'll be up there presently."

Clint nodded and started into the hotel after the two men lugging the chest.

"Oh, by the way," Lane said.

Clint turned.

"You might be interested to know the woman's brother came to town yesterday. Name's Randolph."

"Is that a fact?"

"Yep. Him and me, we had a long talk. He's probably upstairs right now, greeting his sister."

Clint remembered what Loretta had said about her brother, that he'd kill her for what was in the black chest.

Clint ran into the hotel, past the two men who were lugging the heavy chest.

FORTY-SIX

Clint ran down the hall to Loretta's room, slammed the door open and saw two people in the center of the room in a clinch, kissing.

Loretta and . . . her brother?

"Randolph, I presume," Clint said, as the two people leapt apart.

"That's right," the man said. He was tall, handsome, well-dressed in a black suit, in his thirties, and—with his momentary surprise gone—seemed very confident.

"Randolph, this is Clint Adams," she said. "He's the man who got the chest back for us."

"Ah," Randolph said. "Loretta's just been telling me how we almost lost it."

"Yes," Clint said, "quite a coincidence, falling off the back of the stage like that."

"Coincidence? She told me two stage line employees conspired to steal it. Luckily, they couldn't get it open." The man chuckled. "You'd have to use dynamite to do that."

Clint stood there, staring at the two of them. Loretta only had eyes for Randolph, and did not look at Clint once.

"Is there something else we can do for you?" the man asked.

At that moment, the two men arrived carrying the chest.

"Where ya want this?" one of them asked.

"Oh, excellent," Randolph said. "Just put it in that corner."

They did as he asked, then stood there, panting.

"I assume this gentleman has paid you," Randolph said. "That's all."

The two men exchanged a glance, and then trudged from the room.

"This is just a wild guess," Clint said, "but you two are not brother and sister."

"What?" Randolph laughed and looked at Loretta. "Is that what you told him?"

She shrugged and said, "I had to tell them something. I had to convince them there was nothing valuable in the chest."

"Ah, I see," Randolph said.

"So this is about more than a framed photograph."

Randolph laughed again.

"That photo?" He looked at Loretta. "The one of your father?"

"Well," she said, "it has a lot of sentimental value to me."

Clint walked to the window and looked out. Sheriff Lane was in the street, flanked by about five other men. Seemed the sheriff had decided that there was safety in numbers.

"Well, maybe you can convince the sheriff of that," Clint said.

Loretta went to the window and looked out.

"Oh, no," she said.

Randolph joined her.

"What do they want?" he asked.

"The chest," Clint said, "or what's in it. And I mean, what's really in it."

Loretta and Randolph looked at Clint.

"You can't let him come up here and get it, Clint," she said.

"Me? Why should I care? You've obviously been lying to me from the start—about a lot of things."

"I understood you worked for us," Randolph said.

"I was working for Loretta," Clint said. "Actually, I haven't been paid yet. At least, not in money."

Randolph looked at Loretta and said, "Oh?"

"I had to do something to keep him interested," she said. She went to the bed and took the roll of money from her drawstring purse.

"Here," she said to Clint. "A thousand dollars. You have to keep us safe until we can get out of town."

"I don't think so," he said.

"What?" she asked.

"I'm not interested."

"I count six men down there," Randolph said. "And is that the town sheriff?"

"It is," Clint said. "And he's very interested in the chest. Unfortunately, I'm not."

He started out of the room.

"Wait!" Loretta said. She looked imploringly at Randolph.

"I see my love wants to let you in on our little secret."

He walked to the chest, knelt down, touched his hands to each side near the bottom. Suddenly, a drawer slid out from the bottom. He pulled it out farther so Clint could see what was in it.

"That looks like gold," he said.

"Hammered flat as we could get it," Randolph said. "The bottom and the sides are lined."

"That's what makes it so heavy," Clint said.

"And strong," Randolph said. He slid the drawer shut and Clint heard it lock. The man stood up and faced Clint. "I suppose we have to include you, now. A three-way split."

"I'm going to assume it's stolen."

"Does that matter?" Loretta asked. "It's gold!"

"Actually, it doesn't matter," Clint said. "Not to me, anyway. I'm still not interested."

"What?"

Randolph chuckled nervously. "Not interested in an equal split?" the man asked.

"*Any* split."

"There's six men out there," Loretta said. "They'll kill us for this, once they find out what's in it."

"I suppose they will."

"Half," Randolph said, now openly nervous. "Half for you."

"No," Clint said.

"You're crazy, man," Randolph said.

"Maybe," Clint said. "But I'm done."

As he started out, Loretta ran to him and grabbed him.

"You can't," she said. "You can't leave me like this."

"You've got Randolph," Clint said. "He looks competent."

"Not against six gunmen!" she said.

"I'm afraid she's right," Randolph said. "How much can we offer you?"

"You can offer me all of it," Clint said. "I'm still not interested."

He left both of them there, mouths open, gaping after him.

Clint went downstairs, through the lobby, and outside. He walked to his horse.

"Leavin'?" Lane asked.

Clint mounted up and looked down at the sheriff.

"My part's done"

"What's in it?" Lane asked.

"You'll find out," Clint said, "and you'll be pleasantly surprised. But you should know one thing."

"What's that?" Lane asked.

"You can get it without killing them."

"That would be nice," Lane said. "Preferable, in fact."

"Yes," Clint said, "Yes, it would."

He turned Eclipse and rode out of Westbrook.